(megan)

MARY HOOPER

(megan)

MARY HOOPER

BLOOMSBURY

First published in Great Britain in 1999
Bloomsbury Publishing Plc, 38 Soho Square, London, W1V 5DF

Copyright © Text Mary Hooper 1999

The moral right of the author has been asserted
A CIP catalogue record of this book is available from the
British Library

The publishers gratefully acknowledge the following permission to reproduce
the cover image, 'Speak My Mind', photograph by Tracey Chiang, © 1994.
Reproduced by kind permission of Tracey Chiang

ISBN 0 7475 4164 7

Printed in Great Britain by Clays Ltd, St Ives plc

10 9 8 7 6 5 4 3 2

Cover Design by Michelle Radford

To my own first:
Rowan,
to embarrass him

CHAPTER ONE

The lesson was Personal Development.

I was glad about that. Not glad it was that particular subject, I mean, but glad that because it was, the boys weren't in with us. In our school, when we have PD, the boys have extra sport. Maybe they don't need to be developed personally, or maybe they've developed enough. Anyhow, they weren't there and, because of what happened, I was glad.

Miss Springer, who takes us for it, isn't quite a teacher, but a sort of pastoral person who we're supposed to go and talk to if we've got any problems that aren't school problems. To my living knowledge, no one has ever been.

Her lessons are a bit of a doss; Claire and I use them to send notes to each other or do Top Tens: top ten most luscious boys we know or top ten gorgeous TV soap stars and so on. The other thing we do in Miss Springer's lessons is try and make her go red: she's got ginger hair and a pale skin and she blushes really easily, so we set someone up to ask a question: 'Miss Springer, what's oral sex?' or 'Miss Springer, what's an orgasm?' and you get points on how red she goes.

What she was talking about in this particular lesson was female reproduction: periods and the pill and how it affects your body and so on. She was rambling on and I wasn't taking all of it in and then she said, 'Of course, it is possible to be pregnant and still have periods.'

I didn't hear what she went on to after that, I was just stuck on that: *Of course, it is possible to be pregnant and still have periods.*

Claire passed me a note but I didn't look down, just sat staring to the front of the class, where Miss Springer stood, smiling and chatting away, trying to be your favourite auntie. I stared so hard her red hair blurred into a mist: *Of course, it is possible to be pregnant and still have periods.*

Claire nudged me and impatiently jiggled the note up and down on my desk to make me take notice of it.

I looked down. *Top Ten of Records with the Word Love in the Title* I read, but it didn't mean a thing.

Without thinking, my hand moved onto my stomach. It didn't feel any different. But was that because I didn't want it to? Was it just a bit bigger? Rounder? More wobbly?

'There are many different versions of the Pill now and if you do start taking one particular brand and later find that it doesn't agree with you, then do go back to your doctor or clinic,' Miss Springer went on cheerfully.

'I can only think of *five*,' Claire said in a whisper. 'Do you know any more?'

I looked down at the Top Ten again, then back to Miss Springer. Her hair was so frizzy and bright that it almost made me feel sick.

Of course, it is possible to be pregnant and still have periods.

I'd missed one period, last month. I was due on again next week, and I'd decided to go to the doctor or at least mention it to someone if it didn't happen. I wasn't worried, though (that is, I hadn't been worried) because I thought there was no way I could *possibly* be pregnant. How could I be?

It wasn't that I hadn't ever slept with someone: I had, but months ago. I'd slept with someone twice. Not two different boys, I mean, just Luke. But that had been way back in November. We'd split up just after that: I'd seen him snogging with someone else at a Christmas party and we'd had an awful row and I'd finished with him. The whole of January, February and March, Luke and I hadn't spoken to each other, let alone anything else, and I hadn't thought much about when *it* had happened, other than to wish it had been a bit more exciting and to think what a waste of the big occasion – the losing of the virginity occasion – when what we had between us wasn't strong enough or important enough to survive the first row.

I picked up my pen and began to write on the Top Ten list. *November, December, January, February* I wrote down the page, and then I added, *March* and circled it.

'It' had happened in November, and I'd had periods as usual in December, January and February. I'd missed the March one and if I missed this month's as well I'd be . . . I totted it up . . . five months pregnant! My heart began to beat terribly fast and I started to breathe funny: as if I'd just run a race.

Claire peered over my shoulder at the piece of paper. 'What are you doing?' she hissed.

'Miss Springer?' Naomi called from further down the room.

The vague murmurings and noises in the class stopped suddenly, and everyone sat up and looked to the front.

'Yes, Naomi?' Miss Springer asked, sounding wary. 'What is it?'

'What happens when a man changes sex?' Naomi asked, frowning intently. 'How does he actually do it afterwards?'

There were several giggles round the class.

'Well, I . . . er . . . I don't think I've got enough actual information on the er . . . subject to . . . er . . . ' Miss Springer said, going scarlet.

Five months pregnant.

I didn't believe it. Just didn't believe it.

And yet . . . and yet . . .

I thought about the way I'd been feeling – not exactly sick, but sort of groggy in the mornings. And the way I'd completely and utterly gone off greasy food. And the way my bust had gone up a whole cup size, so that I now I actually had a Wonderbra style cleavage without needing the Wonderbra. And there was something else, too . . .

Claire nudged me again, harder. 'What's up with you?' she asked, as Miss Springer, failing to tell us what transsexuals did in bed, moved quickly onto another subject and wrote on the board: *Hormones: Oestrogen and Progesterone.*

I looked at Claire blankly.

'You're supposed to be writing titles with love in them,' she said, scribbling out my own list of months. 'Are you coming along to the square tonight?'

'Dunno,' I muttered.

The something else – well, I'd tried not to think about it, but when I'd had a period in December I'd been *so* relieved. The something else was: when we'd done it the first time, *we hadn't used anything*. Luke had said that he'd withdraw in time, that it would be all right, nothing would happen, none of the little wriggly tadpole things would get in and make me pregnant. That's what he'd said, and I'd believed him.

All those things, though, added together, came to one *big* thing. If I didn't come on next week, then it was true.

I tried to work it out in my head, counting on my fingers under cover of the desk: if I was five months pregnant now, in April, then I'd have a baby in August.

My heart felt as if it was about to go into overdrive. *A baby.*

It couldn't really be true.

I wanted to back-track and ask Miss Springer more about this having periods and still being pregnant

12

business, but I couldn't do that now we'd moved on to other things. Everyone would think I was weird. Everyone would start thinking things.

But they were going to think things anyway. In a couple more months, when I was the size of an elephant, they'd not only think things, they'd know things. Everyone in the world would know that I, Megan Warrell, was an unmarried mother. Claire, Luke, Mum and my sister Ellie, the girls at school, relations, the teachers, the doctors, the people in the shops, the neighbours, people in the street, the whole world would know.

And I was taking my GCSEs in June, as well. And Claire and I had planned to go away together this summer, and it was my 16th birthday at the beginning of September and I was supposed to be having a big party in the garden of the flats where we lived, with lights in the trees and everything.

I put my head on my hands and closed my eyes. Maybe I was dreaming. Maybe it wasn't really happening.

Claire shook me. 'Don't go to sleep!' she hissed. 'What's up with you this morning, anyway?'

I did *not* want a baby. I hated babies. My friend Emily's mum had a baby and it cried and dribbled all

13

the time and there was a little crease in its fat neck where bits of food collected.

If the baby knew I didn't want it, maybe it would go away.

The bell for Break went and Miss Springer carefully rubbed the words *Hormones: Oestrogen and Progesterone* off the board, said we were to look after ourselves and that she'd see us next week.

Naomi came over. 'Did you see how red she went?! Even her ears were blushing.'

'So what *do* they do, anyway?' someone said, and Claire and everyone started laughing.

'They haven't got anything there, have they?' Vinny said. 'They have it all taken away. Every bit of it.'

'But they've got to wee,' Claire said. 'They must have something there to wee with!'

She sounded so indignant about it that I started laughing.

'Well, maybe they have a little something left,' Josie said.

'Yeah!' Naomi said eagerly, 'a teeny, weeny little something!'

I laughed and laughed, doubled over with hysterics, and then I found that there were tears running down my face and I was crying.

'It's not that funny,' said Josie.

Claire leant towards me and looked at me closely. 'You're crying!'

'No, I'm not! Don't be stupid!' I shouted, and I picked up my bag and ran out of the room.

CHAPTER TWO

I went into the library. I didn't think anyone would look for me there. I went straight to the part where the reference books were, into the section called *Health*, and found a hefty book called *Pregnancy and Childbirth*.

In the chapter headed 'Your Baby's Progress and Development', I found drawings of curled up nearly-babies inside women. Underneath were written descriptions of the bits they had according to what month they were.

With a horrible fascination I looked at the five-month one. It said: 'The foetus is now growing with astonishing speed. You can see hair on head and eyebrows. This may be the first month you can hear a heartbeat. The foetus is sleeping and waking at regular intervals, just like a real baby! By the end of this month it will be about the size of a large grapefruit.'

I sat for some moments looking at the weird drawing

on the page. *About the size of a large grapefruit.* Yuk. It might have hair and eyebrows but it didn't look much like a baby to me, more like a cod on a fishmonger's slab. There was no way I wanted one of those inside me.

A picture of Emily's mum's baby, fat, toothless, dribbling, came into my head and I made a little noise of protest. No! I didn't want one of those, either – and I didn't even want one of the smiling, pink ones you see in advertisements for nappies. I didn't want one at all, under any circumstances.

Was one of those things *really* inside me? I put my hand on my tummy again. Could I feel something in there or was I imagining it? Was that just a bit of wobbly fat or something else?

I hesitated for a moment, and then I looked up *Abortion.* I couldn't find that actual word, but I found what I wanted under *Termination.*

When I'd skimmed through the paragraphs I closed the book and put it back on the shelf. It was as I'd thought; as I'd remembered from PD lessons and from different things other girls had told me: five months was too late for an abortion. Summed up, what the book had said was that abortions are fairly uncomplicated under three months, then get more and more tricky and are hardly done at all after four and a half months, except in exceptional cases. And I was five months.

Probably. Only I wouldn't know for definite until next week.

Unless – my heart started racing again – I bought one of those pregnancy kits and did a test. How much were they, though? And where could I go to buy one without anyone seeing me?

There was a sudden clatter of footsteps on the library floor. 'I've been looking everywhere for you!' Claire said, arriving at my side. 'What are you doing in here?'

She glanced up at the name of the section I was in. 'What's wrong? Are you ill or something?'

I shook my head, glad I'd put the Pregnancy book back. Okay, Claire was my best friend and all that, but this was all too awful and too serious and too horrific.

'I just . . . just wanted to find out something. About what Miss Springer told us,' I said.

Claire raised her eyebrows. 'What?'

'It doesn't matter.'

She looked at me oddly. 'Are you coming outside now, then?'

I shook my head again. 'The bell's about to go.'

She scanned the shelves suspiciously, looking for clues as to why I was behaving strangely. Then she said, 'You coming down the square tonight?'

'Not sure,' I said. The square is in the centre of town, about half a mile from the flats where Claire and I both live. If we get fed up with hanging around the flats, and can't afford to see a film or anything, then on a Friday night we quite often go to sit in the square and chat to any boys that might be about. Well, I say chat, but with them it isn't a real chat, not an actual conversation, but a sort of two-way trade of insults. Lately, though, we haven't been along so much. Not since I split up from Luke.

'They're going to be there,' she said. 'Luke and the others. Dave asked me if we were going.' She turned away from me and glanced out of the window. 'D'you think you'll ever get back with Luke?'

I looked at her sharply. 'Why d'you ask?'

She shrugged.

I started to cry again; I just couldn't help it, everything was so near the surface. Now I'd thought about it, worked things out, seen diagrams in the book, it was all so real. It was true, I *knew* it was true.

Claire's jaw dropped and she looked at me, amazed. She plonked herself down on the chair next to me and put an arm round my shoulders. 'What's up? Is there something wrong with you?'

I nodded.

'What?'

The urge to tell her was enormous; Claire and I had always told each other everything, including the rude bits – *especially* the rude bits. But I still hesitated. This wasn't just something to giggle about.

'What've you got, then?' she asked. 'It can't be that bad. How d'you know you've got it?'

'I think I'm . . . pregnant,' I said slowly.

A long moment went by. I wasn't even sure if she'd heard me. Then she said, '*What?*'

I didn't say it again, just sat there crying.

'But you said you . . . How *can* you be? You haven't been out with Luke so you haven't done anything lately and . . . ' Her eyes nearly popped out of her head. 'Here, you haven't done it with anyone else, have you?'

'No, I haven't!' I said irritably. I reminded her what Miss Springer had said, although Claire said she hadn't heard it in the first place. 'So if you can still have periods,' I finished, 'then I can be, quite easily.'

Claire's eyes grew wide and her mouth gaped. 'What will you do?'

'Dunno.'

'Will you marry him, d'you think?'

'Don't be mad.'

The bell went for end of Break.

'But you can have an abortion or something, can't you?' she urged. 'You don't have to have it, do you?'

I shook my head. 'I've just looked it up. You can't have abortions after four and a half months.'

'Oh.' Claire breathed deeply, staring at me. There was shock in her face, but something else as well. Not just sympathy . . . but something like that German word that means being secretly pleased about someone else's misfortune, because if it's happened to them, it's not so likely to happen to you. 'I can't believe it!' she said.

'*You* can't!'

She took another inward gasp of breath. 'What will your mum say? She'll kill you!'

I shook my head wordlessly. *Mum*. What a nightmare.

We heard footsteps and the librarian looked around the corner at us. 'You two still here? The bell's gone, you know.'

'We're just going,' Claire said. She nudged me and bent down to pick up my bag. 'Come on. We've got double Maths with Miss Mays.'

'I'm not going,' I said. 'I can't think about Maths. I'm going to bunk off. Tell Maysie I've got a dentist's appointment or something.'

'Where're you going, then?'

'Home to get some money and then I'm going to buy one of those pregnancy kits.'

'Wow!' she breathed. 'How d'you do them? D'you get the result straight away? Shall I see you later so you can tell me what it said?' she asked eagerly.

I nodded.

'Or ring me. We'll have to talk in code,' she said, her eyes gleaming. 'This is *so* big, we've got to make sure that no one else finds out yet. This is like . . . top secret.'

I stared at her. 'There's no need to sound so bloody pleased about it!'

'I wasn't!'

I started crying again. Or maybe I hadn't stopped from the last time, I don't know. Either way, everything felt utterly hopeless and the worse thing that could ever happen to anyone in the world.

Claire walked with me to the school door.

'You wouldn't . . . Don't say anything to anyone, will you?' I said as she turned to go back into class.

'Of course not!' she said.

'I mean . . . there might be a way. Or perhaps I'm *not*.'

She nodded. 'Good luck,' she said. 'See you later.'

I've heard people say that their feet dragged and felt like lead when they walked – and that's how mine felt walking out of school that afternoon. I avoided looking at the Sixth Form block; that was on the other side of the playground and where Luke was. What was *he* going to say? Should I tell him? He'd find out even if I didn't. And anyway, it was his fault, wasn't it? He'd said he'd pull out in time, that nothing would happen . . .

Going out through the gates felt pretty different from going in through them that morning. Then my only thoughts had been of what Claire and I were going to do at the weekend and whether I still fancied Luke or not and whether, if he was suddenly to come at me with two enormous bunches of flowers (dream on), I might go back to him.

Now, apart from my feet dragging, I had a dull ache in the pit of my stomach and a feeling like there was a big stone on my shoulders, weighing me down.

As I walked, I thought three things over and over:

How *could* it have happened?

What had I ever done to deserve something so awful?

What was Mum going to say?

CHAPTER THREE

The test was positive. I was pregnant.

My legs wobbled and I sat down heavily on the side of the bath, staring at the two blue lines. I picked up the leaflet again and reread the awful words: 'Two blue lines as indicated is a positive result for pregnancy. You should now make an appointment to see your doctor.'

I heard a noise in the hall outside as my sister Ellie let herself into the flat and fell over my bag and coat, which I'd dropped on the floor in my hurry to get into the bathroom.

'Megan? Why are you in early?' Ellie called. I heard her walk up to the room we shared. 'Where are you?'

I tried to compose myself. 'In the loo,' I called back.

'How long have you been in?'

'Only a couple of minutes.'

'I didn't see you ahead of me. How come you finished early?'

'I just *did*,' I said. I was in no mood for her and her questioning of me. She was like a miniature version of Mum: ten, going on thirty, and turning out to be all the things I wasn't. She was Miss Goody-Two-Shoes at school – good in lessons *and* well-behaved – and neat and tidy at home, forever cleaning up her side of the bedroom so that my side would show up even worse. She wore little girl clothes; whatever Mum bought her, she liked, and to put the lid on it she hated pop music and thought any bands I liked were disgusting. All in all, she was turning out to be a right little prig.

If Ellie was like Mum, I, apparently, was like our dad (as Mum never ceased to remind me). After he and Mum had split up he'd gone to live in Australia, though, so I had no way of knowing if I really was. Ellie and I heard from him a few times a year; he'd write us long, boring letters and send birthday presents, and sometimes he rang us. Whenever he rang he reminded us that we could go and visit him and his new wife and two children whenever we wanted, although he never sent the money for the ticket.

I heard Ellie's voice very close to the bathroom door. 'What are you doing in there?'

I jumped, and hastily began picking up my bits and pieces. 'What d'you think?'

'Well, hurry up. I want to go!'

Carefully I put everything from the kit back into the box, then checked the floor to make sure I hadn't left any leaflets around. Ellie was like a terrier; she found lost objects, poked her nose into things which didn't concern her and sniffed out other people's secrets. There was nothing she liked more than discovering someone, especially me, breaking some petty rule or other.

I put the box under my jumper and went out, pushing past Ellie without looking at her. I went straight into our bedroom and hid it in my chest of drawers, right at the bottom in the dark space at the back. Then I laid down on my bed and closed my eyes, pretending I was asleep.

I'd have given anything to have my own room. I really needed it now; I felt I needed to pace about, shout, rock backwards and forwards and generally cry, yell and make a fuss about what had happened to me. And another part of me wanted to get right inside myself and be quiet, try and sort things out in my head.

I couldn't do any of that, though. I just had to be normal, so Ellie wouldn't think anything was wrong.

What to do next? Tell Mum? Tell the doctor? Tell Luke? Tell the school? Questions raced about my head. What about my exams – those exams which, in Mum's eyes, were going to be my entrance into another world? Suppose I couldn't take them? What was everyone at school going to say? What was I going to do with a *baby*?

I thought back. As far as I could remember, there had only been one girl at our school who'd got pregnant. Maybe there had been more but they'd left and no one had known about them. The girl's name was Izzy Clark; it had happened two years ago and she'd been in Year 10, the same as I was now. Izzy had been quite plump anyway, so no one had known she was pregnant until she was about seven months. Then there were these frantic whisperings: was she or wasn't she, and who was the father, and how did she have the *nerve* to come to school. Whenever she appeared in the dining hall or playground everyone just *stared* at her. She had her own little group of friends who stuck around her but sometimes the boys had called 'Slag!' after her and yelled 'Izzy's up the duff!' and things like that.

I'd joined in all the whisperings and the rumours, of course, but I'd never shouted after her. I was glad about that now.

About two weeks after everyone found out that she

was pregnant for definite, she disappeared, never to return to school again. Last year someone swore that they'd seen her in Leeds, with twins.

I heard Ellie come into the bedroom but I kept my eyes closed. She changed out of her school uniform and then she went into the kitchen: she likes to make tea for Mum, who comes in about half an hour after us. Sometimes she makes her a sandwich, too, or even, if she's being particularly girlie, a cake. She tries to be Mum's favourite, but I don't know why she bothers because she is, anyway, without all the tea and cake making business.

The phone rang and Ellie answered it. She called out that it was Claire, for me.

'Tell her I'll ring her later,' I said.

Ellie called out again, 'She wants to speak to you *now*.'

I didn't reply and a moment later Ellie's head appeared round the door. 'Why don't you want to speak to her?'

'I just . . . ' My voice trailed away. I didn't want to speak about what Claire wanted to speak about. I wanted to lie on the bed and pretend it wasn't happening. 'I'll ring her later,' I said. 'If you must know, I don't feel very well. I'm lying down.'

Ellie goggled at me, but went to convey this to Claire. When she put the phone down she called to me, 'Have you two had a row, then?'

'Mind your own business,' I snapped.

'No need to take that attitude,' she said in a fair imitation of Mum's voice.

I sighed, suddenly wondering about my dad and what *he* was going to say. I looked over at the photo of him on my bedside table. I keep it there partly to remind myself that I've actually got a dad, and partly because I know it annoys Mum. It's of him when he was about twenty, on holiday with his sister, our Auntie Lorna. We used to see quite a lot of her when we were little, but then she and Mum had some kind of falling out and later she moved away to live in Chester. Pity, really. She's about the only other relative we've got.

Mum came in at four o'clock, same time as usual, and Ellie called that tea was ready so I braced myself, got up and went down to the kitchen. Mum works in an estate agents: she calls herself a negotiations' agent, but actually she just types up the details of the houses. This 'negotiations' agent' business just about sums my mother up: she always tries to pretend we're better than we are. Like, our name's Warrell and she pronounces it Warrell because she thinks it sounds better, and she always refers to our flat as an apartment, and she gets round the fact that we can't afford a car by pretending she's Green and doesn't want to harm the environment. There are a million other things like this which she does, which really drive me mad.

I don't look like her at all. Apart from the fact that she's 45 (although as she's always telling us, she doesn't look it), she's quite small, with short fair hair, neat features and blue eyes. Ellie's the same build as her and has short fair hair, too, but I've got thick dark hair and brown eyes and I'm taller and bigger all over. Sometimes I feel like a great big cuckoo that's been put into a nest that's too small for it.

'You haven't changed your uniform,' Mum said as soon as she saw me. She and Ellie looked at me disapprovingly. 'If you wear that skirt non-stop it'll go all shiny at the back, you know.'

I shrugged. As if I cared about *that*.

'What sort of a day have you had? Have you got your exam dates yet?'

'Not yet,' I said.

Ellie poured out the tea and lifted a plate to indicate the sandwich ready for Mum underneath.

'Lovely, darling!' Mum said. Ellie smiled at me smugly.

'What lessons have you had, Megan?' Mum asked. 'What have you found out today?'

The two little blue lines on the pregnancy testing kit seemed to dance in front of my eyes. I wanted to say: I found out that it's possible to be pregnant and still have periods. How about *that* for finding something out?

'Oh, nothing much,' I said instead. 'Quite boring, really.'

'I can't understand why you haven't been given an exam timetable yet.'

'No, nor can I,' I said automatically. Exam dates. I wished – *how* I wished – that that was all I had to worry about.

CHAPTER FOUR

'You didn't tell your mum, then?' Claire asked. It was the following day, Saturday, and I was at Claire's flat. I'd told her all about the pregnancy testing kit and she was giving me the full *ohmygawd* open-eyed, gaspy mouth treatment.

'You're kidding. Course I didn't. I mean, I'm still here, aren't I?'

'When are you going to, then?'

'Dunno. It's not exactly easy to bring something like that up, is it?'

'And are you *sure*, now? Is that kit a hundred per-cent accurate?'

'I'm sure,' I said.

She plunged into the back of her wardrobe, trying to find something to wear to go shopping in. When she emerged with a washed-out denim shirt she said, 'Do you want me to come with you – help you tell her?'

I looked at Claire: there it was again: the eager tone, the bright eyes. 'That's okay,' I said. 'I'll do it.'

'But you can't leave it much longer, can you?' Her glance went downwards. 'If you're five months you'll be showing soon.'

'I know.' I'd looked at myself very closely in my own wardrobe mirror that morning, while Ellie was having a bath. Suddenly, my bust seemed enormous and the bits round my nipples looked different, browner. My waistline was also definitely fatter, although I could still get my jeans on.

I didn't want to even *think* about telling Mum, though. Apart from the aggro in store, all the while she didn't know I could pretend to myself that it wasn't happening. Like, last night, after Claire had rung again (and been put off again), I'd sat down to watch the comedy programmes on TV and had actually managed to forget all about it. Pregnant? Me? Don't be ridiculous. For a while it all seemed utterly fantastical and bizarre.

Once Mum knew, though, it wouldn't be possible to push it away. There would be shock-horror and drama, then I expected fights and rows and recriminations, followed by doctors and hospitals and internal examinations and all that horrible stuff.

'And . . . like . . . you don't feel you're coming on at all?'

I shook my head. It ought to have been that week-end, but I didn't have any tell-tale tummy ache or that low-down pain you sometimes get in your back just before it happens. I'd *love* that dragging ache and miserable gut feeling now, I thought.

Claire pulled on the denim shirt, took it off again and put on the black sweatshirt she'd had on originally. 'Let's go then!'

We went. It was miserable. Talking about the pregnancy again had made it so real that all I could think about was fat, ugly, screaming babies. We walked down into town, past the travel agents, where we always paused to look at the holidays on offer and try and plan where we'd go when our mums eventually let us off on our own. Claire's sister and her friends had gone Inter-railing last year and this sounded fantastic to us. They'd come back with tales of sleeping rough on beaches, cooking breakfast on foreign railway stations and not changing their clothes for two weeks.

What would happen now, though? Would I *ever* be able to go? Who was going to look after the baby? Was I going to keep it? Would it come with us?

We looked at the holidays on offer in the window and discussed whether ten days on a Greek island was preferable to a week in Sardinia, but our hearts weren't in it.

'What about this year?' Claire asked anxiously. 'D'you think you'll still be able to come away with us?'

Claire's mum and dad had booked a two-bedroom chalet for a week in a holiday camp and because her sister was going off with her friends again, they'd asked me along with them. The place had looked quite good from the brochure; there was a clubhouse with a disco and live music, and a huge swimming pool with flumes, and you only had to walk two minutes to get onto the beach.

What now, though?

I counted on my fingers again (not that I needed to, August was kind of etched on my brain). 'We're going in July, aren't we? I'll be eight months pregnant then!'

Her jaw dropped. 'Imagine what you'll look like in a bikini!'

'Like an elephant,' I said.

'That'll be good for picking up lads, eh?' she snorted, and then she paused and said, 'Are you sure you can't get rid of it?'

My hand automatically went down onto my tummy. 'Yeah, I'm sure.'

'Maybe if you went to the doctors *right now*.'

I shook my head. 'I think I would have got rid of it if I'd known earlier, but I'm too scared to do anything like that now.' I hesitated. 'It's quite big, you see. I can't think how it would be. I bet it really hurts if you do it now . . . I read in a book that it's as big as grapefruit.'

She pulled a face. 'Sounds *disgusting*.'

Claire had a *Pizzas R Us* voucher offering two pizzas for the price of one, so after we'd trailed round the shops a bit and tried on a few things, we went to use it.

Pizzas R Us is a huge place but it was crowded in there because everyone was using their vouchers. As soon as we got inside the door Claire clutched me dramatically. 'There's Luke!' she said. 'Oh my God! How d'you feel? D'you want to go?'

I would much rather have turned and gone straight out, but that would have been playing along with Claire somehow, making a fuss, causing a bit of a sensation. 'It might look funny if we run out,' I said in a low voice. 'I've got to face him some time. Besides, he's right over the back with all the others. He might not see us.'

Claire nodded. 'No, he might not.'

Yeah, she *said* that, but then she made a fuss getting

39

to our seats, laughing loudly and making a joke with the waitress on the way over to make sure he did.

They all saw us, of course, and whistled to us. A bit later, when they got up to leave, Claire waved to them, but I didn't. I felt my cheeks flaming; I felt as if they could tell, just by looking at me, that I *was*. And I couldn't bear to look at Luke at all. I hated him – *hated* him – for what he'd done to me. I didn't realise until I saw him how much I hated him.

We sat down and ordered triple cheese pizzas. Claire said, 'There, that was all right, wasn't it? At least you've seen him now.'

I didn't say anything.

'Do you feel funny about him?' she asked. 'Do you feel – I dunno – a sort of link with him because he's the . . . ' her voice lowered, ' . . . father of your baby?'

'Of course I don't!'

'You might . . . I mean, I just thought now this has happened you might want to get back with him again.'

I shook my head vehemently. 'I hate him!'

'Yeah, well you say that now. But you'll have to have some sort of contact because he's got to help you, hasn't he? He's got to give you money and all that. It's the law.'

I looked down at the table and smeared a blob of tomato ketchup right along the glass top. I felt as if I was going to start crying again. How was I going to tell him? What would he say? Suppose – I'd heard of this happening – he said it wasn't his? Suppose he said I'd been with half the lads in the Sixth and they all got up in court and swore it was true? What then? And anyway, how could he give me any money when he wasn't earning any?

'Maybe he'll ask you to marry him. You could marry him before you have it,' Claire said, and this was so stupidly unlikely that I started laughing.

'I'm not sixteen until September!' I said. 'And they don't make wedding dresses in maternity sizes.'

'Well, you can get married afterwards, then!' she said. 'You can have the baby as a page boy. Or a bridesmaid.'

'Luke is doing A levels,' I said. 'He wants to go to university. He told me that he's going to have one of those grotty flats that students have, with bacon stuck on the walls and the bread all green and furry. I'm not going to live in one of those with him. Besides, I hate him,' I added.

'But do you *really*?' she asked intently.

I thought about it. 'I dunno,' I said.

To be honest, I didn't know how I felt about anything any more. It was as if I'd fallen into a black hole where there was nothing else in the world except me and my problems. Or one problem in particular.

CHAPTER FIVE

'Well, honestly,' Mum said indignantly, 'I don't know what's wrong with you lately, I really don't. I only have to say the slightest thing for you to go off the handle.'

Tell her now . . .

Immediately I thought that, my stomach turned over with fright. Ellie was upstairs, out of the way, so I *could* tell her now. I *ought* to tell her now. It was an excellent time to tell her.

I nearly giggled when I thought that. An excellent time. Whenever was it an excellent time to tell your mum that you were expecting a baby?

It was Saturday and a week had gone by. A week when (a) I hadn't come on, (b) I'd done another pregnancy test which had come out the same as before and (c) I'd grown fatter by the minute.

It seemed to me that the minute I'd found out I was pregnant, the flab had started to go on. I could no longer wear my jeans, for a start. Or I could, but I had to leave the top button and half the zip undone. All in a week! Other changes were that I kept having to wee, and I had horrible heartburn in the back of my throat whenever I ate anything greasy.

I'd found a baby book in the public library with a page on how to calculate the date of a baby's birth. It had worked out to August 19th. The book had added that it was particularly wearisome carrying a baby over the summer, as apart from dragging a huge weight around, a woman's cooling system often went haywire, which made the heat especially trying for her.

Well, cheers, I thought. Not only was I having a baby that I didn't want, but it was being born at the worst time of the year.

'And I do wish you'd do something about your hair!' Mum said, putting a mug of tea in front of me. 'It never looks clean nowadays.'

That was another thing: my hair had gone all greasy and lank and I really needed to wash it every day to keep it looking halfway decent.

'I washed it yesterday,' I said, running my fingers through it.

'You should have it cut short again. Really suited you short,' Mum said. 'You looked very smart.'

'I looked like a nerd,' I said.

'If being a nerd is being smart and tidy, then I'm all for it. You'll never get a holiday job if you look scruffy. That was half the trouble with your father, you know; he never looked really well-groomed.'

You'll never get a holiday job if you're eight months pregnant, I thought.

Tell her. I took a gulp of tea and glanced anxiously towards the door, wondering how long Ellie was going to be upstairs.

'And while we're on the subject of clean and tidy, I do hope you're not going to wear those awful jeans again. They look as if they've got axle grease on them. And so ripped!'

'It took me ages to get them like that,' I said. 'Don't do anything to them, will you?'

'What? Like scrub them? I wouldn't waste the energy!'

Oh God . . . I closed my eyes, took a deep breath – and heard Ellie running down the stairs.

I breathed out hard. Never had I been so pleased to see her.

'I was just coming up with your tea,' Mum said to her fondly. 'Finished tidying up your side of the bedroom, have you?'

As Ellie started listing all the things that were a mess on *my* side, I took another gulp of tea and then got up. 'I think I'll go down to Claire's.'

I didn't go to Claire's. For one thing it was too early – and for another I just didn't want to talk to anyone. Anyway, I *knew* Claire would immediately ask me whether I'd told Mum or not. She asked every day and it was stressing me out.

I caught the bus and went into town on my own – and that was where I bumped into Luke.

He was just coming out of the chemist's; I think he'd been in there getting shopping for his mum because he had a bag with a packet of eight pink loo rolls in it. When he saw me he tried to hide it behind his back.

My heart started beating like the clappers but, in spite of knowing that I should talk to him, that I desperately *needed* to talk to him, I just nodded and rushed on by, as if I was in a mad hurry to get some-where.

He caught hold of my arm as I went past, though. I tried to shake it off, but he held it firmly.

'Aren't you speaking to me, then?'

I swallowed. Didn't answer. Looked at the ground.

'Come on, this is stupid,' he said. 'We see each other practically every day. We ought to be able to say hello.'

I looked at him, feeling wobbly, and he loosened his grip on my arm slightly. 'You OK?'

I shook my head.

'What's the matter?' His hand dropped away. 'Look, I didn't mean to freak you out or anything. I just felt we ought to be able to say hello to each other.'

I still didn't speak.

'Shall I just sod off?'

'No,' I said. I had to tell him – and after all, it was his fault just as much as mine. It was his fault *more* than mine. I glanced up and down the street. 'I do want to speak to you.'

'Good.'

My heart was thudding. 'No, I mean speak about something in particular.'

His eyebrows lifted and I reckoned I knew what he was thinking: that I wanted to go back with him.

'Do you want to walk or something?' he asked.

I nodded. 'Let's just go down to the river.'

We began to walk past the shops and across the big car park towards the river. We'd walked down there in the past, when we'd been going out together. There were ducks and a bridge and willow trees; it was quite pretty.

We just talked about ordinary things. Some boys are difficult to talk to, but Luke and I have never had any trouble chatting. He's got two sisters, so he's good at talking to girls.

We reached the middle of the bridge and stopped. I leant over it and looked down into the water. I hadn't thought of how to be with him: I didn't know if I should be aggressive, angry, matter-of-fact, tearful, demanding or wimpish. Which of these things did I feel? I wasn't sure.

I swallowed. My heart was going all pittery-pattery, but it didn't feel anywhere near as bad as when I'd tried to tell Mum.

I turned to look at him. 'I'm having a baby,' I said, straight out, and it was such a relief to say it that I began to shake all over.

His mouth gaped. '*What?*'

'I'm expecting a baby and it's due on August 19th.'

'Is it . . . ? Is it mine . . . ?' he stuttered.

I nodded. 'Of course it is.' I didn't feel offended: the question was fair enough. We hadn't slept together for months and after all, he hadn't been at the PD class.

'Apparently you can be pregnant and still have periods – I only found this out a week ago.' I looked at his face; he'd turned quite pale. 'Yeah, I was shocked, too.'

'But . . . When d'you think . . . ?'

'I reckon it happened that first time,' I said.

'Oh, Christ.' He gripped my arm. 'I said I'd . . . '

'Yeah,' I nodded, 'you did. You couldn't have, though, could you?'

He ran his hand through his hair. 'Christ,' he said again. 'I'm really sorry.' There was a long silence and then he said, 'So how pregnant are you?'

'I had three periods when I wasn't supposed to, and now I've missed two, so I'm about five months.'

'*Christ!*'

I looked at him, and I didn't feel aggressive or angry or any of those things. I felt a bit sorry for him, actually. I knew it was him who'd actually got me pregnant in the first place – but then again I'd actually let him. And I'd had enough PD lessons and read enough books to know that you shouldn't even *think* about doing it without protection. That even messing about in that area was risky.

'God, Megan, I'm really, really sorry,' he said, and he looked it, too – I thought he was going to cry. 'What d'you want me to do?'

I shrugged. 'Dunno. Don't know what I'm doing myself.'

'A *baby*. I can't believe it.' He shook his head slowly. 'A *baby*.'

'Yeah – and it's too late for an abortion, by the way, if that's what you're thinking.'

'I'm not thinking anything,' he said shakily. 'It's all too . . . I can't take it in.'

'Nor can I,' I said.

His eyes suddenly filled with alarm. 'What's your mum said?'

'Not a lot,' I said, 'because she doesn't know yet. I haven't got round to telling her.' I pulled a face. 'You know what she's like.'

Luke had only met her a couple of times. Once she'd made him go through his last exam results, wanting to know what A Levels he was taking and why, and once she'd lectured him on bringing me home on time and told him that he wasn't ever to let me have a drink, not even at a party.

'Look,' he said, 'What can I . . . D'you want some money or something?'

I shrugged. 'I don't know. I don't know what I'll need or what I'm going to do or anything.'

'Who knows about . . . about it?'

'Only Claire.'

'What's she say?'

'Not a lot,' I said. 'Mostly she just sits there looking at me with her mouth open.'

'Yeah.' He shook his head. 'Know how she feels.'

We stared down into the water. I heard Luke take a deep breath. 'D'you want . . . D'you want us to sort of get back together?' he asked.

'Just because I'm pregnant?' I shook my head. 'I don't think that would be any good, do you? I mean, you weren't going to ask me anyway, were you?'

'S'pose not,' he said. 'Just thought I ought to mention it.'

'Well, thanks,' I said, and I managed a bit of a smile. One half of me wished that he'd said that he loved me madly and would look after me and take care of me – and the other half knew that was soppy and unrealistic and it wouldn't work anyway.

'I'll help you if I can,' he said, 'with money and so on. I'll be getting some sort of job in the holidays, after the mocks.'

I nodded. 'OK.'

He cleared his throat. 'Look, d'you want me to come round and see your mum with you?'

I smiled again at the thought of Mum set loose on

Luke. 'That's okay,' I said. 'I don't hate you that much.'

He looked at me hard. 'D'you hate me at all?'

'Yeah. No. I dunno.' I sighed. 'I don't know anything any more. I'm just a woolly bundle.'

'What's that mean?'

'I just feel all . . . *woolly*,' I said, unable to explain it further.

There was another long silence, and then Luke said, 'Will you have . . . Will it be adopted, d'you think?'

I shook my head slowly, wondering. *Adoption*: give the baby away. The notion leapfrogged ahead: maybe I could go off somewhere now, right now, and stay there, wherever it was, until I had the baby, and then have it adopted and come home again. Mum needn't ever find out I'd been pregnant . . .

But where would I go? I didn't have any money, not even enough for the rail fare to London, because I'd spent it all on pregnancy tests.

'I just don't know,' I said. 'I don't know anything.'

We spoke a bit more and I left Luke in town – left him standing on the bridge – and went back home. I couldn't face Mum and the continual *screaming* urge to tell her, so I went to Claire's.

'I've just rung you!' she said. 'Have you told your mum?'

I shook my head.

'Only she sounded a bit offish when I asked to speak to you. I wondered if she knew.'

'She'll sound more than offish when she finds out,' I muttered.

Claire ushered me into her bedroom. Their flat is bigger than ours, so she has one to herself.

'I've told someone, though,' I said, sitting down on her bed. 'I've told Luke.'

She gave a short scream. 'Where did you see him . . . Did you arrange to . . . What did he *say*?!'

I shrugged. 'He swore a lot.'

'Was he surprised?'

'Course he was. After all this time he thought he'd got away with it, didn't he?'

'But was he all right about it? Was he nice to you?'

I nodded. 'He was all right. He asked me if I wanted to go back with him.'

She gasped. 'What did you say to that?'

'I said no. He was only asking because he feels guilty.'

'He might not be,' she said, and then she got up and flung open her wardrobe doors. 'I don't know what to wear to Sixth Form disco. What're you going to wear?'

I looked at her in astonishment. 'I haven't even thought about it.'

'Oh no,' she said. 'Of course you haven't. I forgot.'

She'd forgotten. I began crying again. Everything seemed so hopeless. There was just me, with this thing inside, this squirmy grapefruit-sized thing, all alone.

CHAPTER SIX

'You're *fat*!' Ellie said, looking at me with her face screwed up in disgust.

I hastily pulled my T-shirt down over the small bulge which was now my tummy. 'No, I'm not. Anyway, you're too thin.'

'Mum says thin is healthy.'

I made a sneery face – but turned away so that Ellie couldn't see it. She was a right little sneak at telling Mum things like that, and I was trying to keep Mum sweet at the moment while I worked out the best way to tell her.

It was Friday night and – God help me – I was in my bedroom getting ready for the school disco. The Sixth Form were allowed to have two discos a year and invite years 9 and 10, so this one was a last fling before everyone got down to exams. I didn't really want to go, but it would have looked strange if I hadn't turned up. Besides, Luke would be there, of course, and I felt funny about that – about not being there when he was around my friends. OK, he'd seemed sensible enough about it, quite straight, but I wasn't sure if I trusted him. If I wasn't at the disco he might say something, ask why I hadn't turned up and grin knowingly. He might drop a hint to someone or boast about it to a mate. If he was going to do anything like *that*, I wanted to be there. I hated the thought of everyone gossiping behind my back.

'I hope you're going to hang those clothes up,' Ellie said, looking disapprovingly at the heap of things falling off the end of my bed.

'They're in my half of the room,' I said shortly. There was a pile of trousers that I'd tried to get into but couldn't and half a dozen tops that had looked too skimpy and revealing. It was mad: I'd wanted a proper bust for years, but now I had one I hated it.

'They look all *messy* left in a heap there,' she said with a whine in her voice.

I gritted my teeth, glowered at her and went out. As if I cared about clothes on the end of a bed.

I went round for Claire. She was wearing tight black trousers and a white bra-top thing made out of shiny, stretchy stuff. She's got olive skin – her dad is Spanish – so she always looks good in white.

I looked at her and sighed. 'This huge T-shirt was

56

all I could get into,' I said. 'And my jeans are undone all the way down with a big safety pin holding them together.'

She looked at me critically. 'You look like Jo Brand,' she said.

'I don't care.'

'You haven't told her yet, then?'

'Mum?' I shook my head. 'I wouldn't be here if I had. She'd have killed me by now.'

She gave me a little shake. 'Well, never mind her now,' she said. 'Cheer up! We're supposed to be going to a disco, not a funeral.'

'I thought you said he was all right about it. Thought you said he was nice to you?'

'He was.'

Claire looked over my shoulder to where, behind me, Luke was chatting to Naomi and April.

'Well, he's not now, is he? He hasn't taken any notice of you since you got here. He hasn't even said hello.'

'So?' I felt hot and irritable. We were standing by the 'bar' of the disco – which was actually a table selling non-alcoholic drinks – my back ached and there was loud music coming out of a speaker right by my ear.

'Well, it's not very nice, is it? You'd think he'd make a bit of a fuss of you. After all you are . . . '

'All right, all right!' I said. 'I do know, thank you very much.'

'Shall I go and have a word with him?'

'Don't you dare!'

'Well, it doesn't seem right. There he is chatting up Naomi and you're . . . '

'For God's sake!' I exploded. 'Let me worry about it, will you? It's nothing to do with you.'

I felt a bit peed off with the situation, with *him*, but then again I didn't fancy him now anyway. Fancying him, come to think of it, had only lasted about three months. If I'd known it was only going to last that long, I wouldn't have done it.

I tried to think back to how I'd felt about him at first . . . how I'd felt when we'd done it. I'd thought that I loved him, I suppose. I'd been mad about him, couldn't stop thinking about him – was that love? How was I to know that the feeling wouldn't last, though? That by the time I'd seen him snogging Lisa at a party I'd have been (secretly) quite pleased to have the excuse to finish it between us.

That was a bit worrying, actually: I'd had three boyfriends so far in my life and the feelings that I'd had for the other two hadn't lasted either. Suppose, then, I never fancied anyone for more than three months at a time? Suppose my feelings just disappeared like magic after that? Suppose I went through life not having any proper, long-term relationships at all?

Unconsciously, my hand went onto my stomach again . . . How was I going to have boyfriends once I had a baby, anyway? Where would the baby be? Would I take it on dates? Try as I might, I couldn't think of me, with a real live baby, pushing it in a pram. It just could *not* be possible . . .

'Why are you standing like that,' Claire hissed, 'with your hand on your . . . your *you know*?'

I whipped my hand away. 'Shall we go and sit down?' I said.

'In a minute. I want to keep my eye on Luke for you. See what he's up to with Naomi. He definitely fancies her, you know.'

'So what!?' I said, irritated all over again.

Vinny and Josie came up, laughing.

'What are you two on about?' Vinny said above the music. 'You look like you're having a row or something.'

I shrugged.

'We're just going to sit down,' Claire said. Then she added in a loaded way, 'Megan wants to.'

Josie grabbed my hand. 'Oh, don't sit down!' she said. 'Come and dance with us!'

'All right,' I shrugged. I didn't want to, but I didn't want them to think anything if I didn't dance. Besides, maybe jumping about a bit on the dance floor would . . . sort of . . . dislodge something.

Claire looked at me. 'D'you think you ought to dance?' she asked in a concerned voice.

I glared at her.

'Why shouldn't she dance?' Vinny asked curiously.

'Oh, no reason! Nothing,' Claire said, but it was the way she said it. With a secret smile and a sort of *I know something that you don't* look. I wanted to kill her.

The four of us had a few dances – with Claire flinging herself about all over the place – and then there was a half-time break for the DJ, and Vinny and Josie went off to the loo. Claire said she had to go and speak to someone, and before I could ask who, she'd disappeared. When I looked round to see where she was, I saw her standing in the doorway talking to Luke.

I fumed, wondering what she was saying. I could have gone up to them but I felt awfully conspicuous, as if everyone would look at me if I did. I sat on the edge of a chair, trying to arrange my big T-shirt so that all the bagginess was in the front and nothing clung to my stomach.

She was with him about ten minutes.

'Why did you go over there?' I asked crossly when she came back.

She looked at me with an earnest expression. 'We were just talking about you,' she said. 'I know you didn't want me to, but I thought I ought to. I mean, we're the only two people in the world who know, aren't we?'

I felt myself going red, struggling not to get into a temper. 'What did you say to him?'

'Oh, we were just talking about what a shock it all was. He feels really guilty, you know.'

'He doesn't look it.'

'Well, I said that. I said it wasn't very nice of him to chat up Naomi in front of you, and he said he doesn't fancy Naomi, he was just being friendly. So that's all right, isn't it?'

'All right for who?' I said, suddenly suspicious.

'Well, for you, of course. I mean, you don't want . . . '

It suddenly hit me. 'You like him yourself, don't you? You fancy him!'

'Of course I don't!' she said hotly.

'You said once that he was the best-looking boy in his year,' I said, remembering. 'He was in your Top Ten.'

'So?' Now it was her turn to go red. 'That doesn't mean I fancy him. I don't! How bizarre can you get? God, I wouldn't suddenly fancy the boy that you're having a baby with, would I?'

'You might,' I said.

Once the DJ started playing records again we danced a bit more, and then, feeling miserable, I made an excuse and went home early, walking back to the flats with another girl.

I was really off Claire: cross for what she'd said in front of the others, and furious because she'd gone to chat to Luke. OK, I didn't fancy him any more, but that didn't mean I wanted my best friend to start making a play for him, did I?

I lay awake for ages, worrying about everything. I had to tell Mum soon. I *had* to.

I even thought about running away – and then I remembered that Mum had always said to me and Ellie that we could *never* do anything so bad that we had to run away. She'd told us that it would kill her if either of us disappeared . . . that it was the very worst thing that any child could do to their mum.

So maybe getting pregnant *wasn't* the worst thing after all. And anyway, I *had* to tell her. And soon.

CHAPTER SEVEN

Mum stared at me, her eyes hard and grey as rocks. '*What?*' she said. '*What?* I don't believe I heard you correctly.'

I leant against the table in the kitchen, staring at the pattern on the floor.

'You did hear correctly,' I mumbled.

'*What?*' she said again. 'Speak up.'

I gave a mighty sigh. Another week had gone by: a week in which Claire had asked me every single day if I'd told Mum, and a week in which I lived, ate, slept, *dreamed* about telling her. In the end I'd just gone downstairs and come out with it.

'I'm having a baby,' I repeated in a low voice. 'I'm very sorry but I am.'

'You're having a baby and you're *sorry*!' She drew in her breath in a long, shocked gasp. 'Well, how *dare* you!'

I looked up. It wasn't what I was expecting: I was waiting for hysterics or tears or even (as if) a comforting hug.

'Whose is it?'

I shook my head wordlessly.

'Whose *is* it?' she demanded again, and because I didn't answer, this seemed to incense her even more. 'You don't know!' she said, half-hysterical. 'You don't know who the father is!'

I didn't have time to deny this before she was off again.

'How *dare* you do this to me!' She looked at me with fierce cold eyes as if she hated me. 'How dare you do this to our family! What were you thinking of?'

'I didn't do it deliberately,' I said. 'It was an accident.'

'An accident! How can something like that be an accident! A baby! I can't believe it! Oh, how *could* you!'

'Look, I . . . '

She suddenly grasped my arm, wrenched me round to face her properly and looked at my stomach. She put her hand flat on it.

'Oh my God!' she said. 'You wicked girl! You . . . you little slut. Get to your room!'

I gave a hysterical giggle – I just couldn't help it. This was so over-the-top, calling me names and all.

And I hadn't been sent to my room for years and years.

She shook my shoulder. 'Laughing, now! How dare you!'

Tears started in my eyes. I wanted with all my heart for her to put her arms round me and tell me that everything would be all right, that she'd look after me and make it better.

She wasn't that sort of mum, though.

'You heard me!' she said. 'Get out!'

I went straight out of the kitchen and ran to my bedroom. Ellie had gone to a friend's house for tea that day, so I just threw myself on the bed and crawled under the duvet.

I hadn't had any idea of how Mum would react. I knew it would be an awful shock, of course, but it hadn't occurred to me that she might take it personally, like it was an affront to *her*. She always prided herself on being modern, too: talking about AIDS and gays and transvestites and the like as if we mixed with them on a regular basis – but now she had a chance to be really modern and liberated she was behaving like one of those Victorian fathers in paintings who turned their pregnant daughters out into the snow.

I cried for some minutes, rocking myself backwards and forwards in bed and feeling sick and miserable, then there was a noise in the hall and my door was flung open.

'Get up!' Mum said curtly. 'We're going out.'

I looked over the duvet at her. 'Where to?'

'To the doctor's. I've made an emergency appointment for you.'

'It's not worth it,' I said. 'I've done pregnancy tests myself and they were positive.'

'I want to know how far on you are.'

I wiped my eyes on my duvet cover. 'I can tell you that. I'm about five months.'

'Five months!' she said, horrified. '*Five months!* Why didn't you say something before?'

'I didn't know . . . I was still having periods.'

'How long have you known?' she snapped.

'For definite? About three weeks.'

Her face twitched. 'It still might not be too late. Get *up*, I said!'

I got up. It seemed best not to argue. Anyway, although I resented her taking command, in some funny way it made things easier, sort of took some of the responsibility from me. And at least she knew now . . .

I thought she'd lecture me all the way down there. She didn't, though; after leaving the house she didn't speak one word to me, not a single word. We just walked along the pavement in icy silence, a large gap between us. It was like being little again: I remembered that when we'd been out together then and I'd done something which made her cross, she always refused to hold my hand.

Because it was late Friday afternoon we had to have whichever doctor we could get, so we got someone who didn't really belong to our surgery.

I didn't like him. Soon as I saw him I didn't like him. He was a bit older than Mum and had a bow tie and glasses on the end of his nose. He squinted down these to look at me.

After examining me, which was ghastly, he wrote down some dates and said that I was about twenty-two weeks pregnant and that it was 'dangerously close to being too late for a termination'.

'You mean she could still have one?' Mum said.

'Only in extreme circumstances,' said the doctor. He spoke in a posh, impatient voice, not looking at me.

'She's only fifteen – that's extreme in my book,' Mum said.

'But not medically speaking,' he said.

I just sat there while they spoke across me, as if I didn't count at all.

'I'll give you a prescription for vitamin and iron supplements and get the social worker to make an ante-natal appointment at the hospital for you. She'll call on you next week,' the doctor said to Mum.

'Social worker!' Mum said. 'What do we need one of those for? Surely that won't be necessary.' She was horrified; it was as if someone had suggested that the plague cart call.

'It will, I'm afraid, because your daughter is under-age. Also because it's got to be decided where she's going to have the baby – and then decided what will happen to it afterwards. She'll have to be supervised and monitored from now on. All the way along the line,' he added wearily.

'I want you to know that I don't condone this kind of behaviour,' Mum said.

I stared at the wall, at a poster which showed a woman flat on her back with a caption underneath saying: 'Don't take it lying down! Plan your baby!'

'This is the first time anything like this has ever happened in our family,' Mum went on, speaking in her posh estate agent's voice.

The doctor nodded as if he'd heard it all before. 'The social worker will be able to help you as the months go by,' he said.

'She can have it adopted,' Mum said firmly.

The doctor was scribbling down things all the time they were speaking, so I thought I'd better speak up before he wrote *that* down and it became law.

'Hang on,' I said. 'I don't know yet if I want it adopted.'

Mum's eyes hardened. 'You'll do what's best,' she said. 'Who do you think's going to look after it while you're at school? I'm certainly not having it. I've got my career to think of.'

The doctor put down his pen. 'All the details can be worked out later,' he said. He looked through his glasses and down his nose at me. 'You young girls – if only you'd take more care. You don't realise what trouble you're bringing on yourself.'

He looked across at Mum. 'They often do it as a status symbol, you know – to make themselves more important amongst their friends.'

My blood boiled and I felt Mum stiffen. 'I'm not sure that's quite what's happened in my daughter's case,' she said, and I glanced at her. Careful, Mum, I thought. That could almost be taken as a message of support.

'There's lots of peer pressure to sleep around,' he went on.

I gave him a hate-filled look. I wanted to shout 'Bollocks!' or 'What do you know about anything, you cretin?' but I felt too miserable and squashed to make the effort. And I was in enough trouble anyway.

'Will there be any support – either emotional or financial – from the father of the baby?' he asked me.

I shrugged, not knowing what to say.

'Megan?' Mum asked.

'I'm not sure,' I mumbled.

'Speak up!' Mum said. 'It's Luke's, I take it? Got you drunk, did he?'

'No, of course he didn't,' I said, falling straight into the trap of letting her know it was Luke's.

'Well, why didn't you take precautions? Don't they teach you anything at that school?' She gathered breath. 'Oh he'll pay for it, all right!' she said to the doctor. 'I'll make sure of that.'

'The social worker will help you sort out those sorts of details,' he said. He gave a prescription form to Mum, as if she was going to be the one needing it.

Mum, steely-faced, poked me with her finger to get up.

'Thank you very much for seeing us at short notice, doctor,' she said prissily.

'Good afternoon,' he said.

Mum poked me again but I didn't say anything. Why should I?

We walked home in silence. The only time Mum spoke was to look at the prescription and say, 'Iron and vitamin supplements. Of course, everyone in the chemist's will know what's up when I take *this* in.'

'I'll take it to another chemist's, then,' I said.

'The *shame* of it. To think that we've come to this.'

'There are worse things,' I said, thinking about what she'd always said about running away, and about drugs and disease and death and all the other horrible things in the world.

I gnawed over things in my head, and when we got in I said, 'You always used to tell me that there was nothing that was so awful that I couldn't come to you about it. And now . . . now something awful *has* happened and I've come to you, you're carrying on as if – oh, I dunno – as if the world's fallen in or something.'

Mum was hanging her coat up in the hall. She was silent for a while, and when she turned round her face was all twisted and she looked as if she was trying not to cry.

'I wanted so much more for you,' she said. 'You don't realise . . . Bringing you up on my own has been difficult, but I thought I was doing my best, giving you opportunities that I never had and hoping all the time that it would all pay off and you'd make a good life for yourself.'

'Well, I . . . '

'Now you've just thrown it all away. Just for nothing. In one moment of stupidity.'

I opened and shut my mouth a few times, feeling all gormless and tongue-tied. 'It might be all right,' I said limply. 'It doesn't have to be all thrown away, does it? It's not *that* awful.'

'Oh, it is,' she said immediately. 'Believe me, it's as awful as it could possibly be.'

The whole weekend was a nightmare. Mum hardly spoke to me at all, just went about the place being tight-lipped and snappy and only speaking when it was strictly necessary – when someone else was around. In contrast, she was even more cosy and friendly to Ellie, though Ellie didn't seem to notice. I wondered when she was going to be told, and what sort of a meal Mum would make of telling her.

The social worker phoned on Sunday and, Mum said to me in a bitter undertone, would be coming at two o'clock on Monday afternoon, which would mean me coming home from school early and Mum having that afternoon off work. This was like the last blow; she went on at me about important appointments she'd have to miss and special meetings she was supposed to attend. It was like the whole of the property market was going to collapse without her.

Claire phoned that evening, just after Ellie had gone to bed. Mum answered the phone and said, 'For you. I suppose *she* knows, does she? Oh yes, I'm sure the best friend found out before the mother.'

I didn't reply. I stretched the phone line out into the hall to get as far away as I could, so Mum wouldn't hear.

'She knows, doesn't she!' Claire said, sounding horrified and fascinated at the same time.

'You could say that.' I was conscious of Mum listening on the other side of the door.

'Was it awful?'

'Yes.'

'Does that mean everyone at school will have to know now?' Claire asked. A bit too eagerly, I thought.

'No! Look, I'll talk to you about it tomorrow, OK?'

I put the phone down and went upstairs. I wanted to crawl under my duvet and die, I really did.

CHAPTER EIGHT

The following morning, Claire was waiting for me outside the flats.

'What did she say? Was it terrible? Did she go mad?'

'You could say that,' I said. 'Mad and cold and horrible. As if I'd murdered someone. And then she marched me down the surgery and I had to see an awful doctor.'

I began telling her all about it, and by the time I'd finished we'd reached the school gates. I shut up then and changed the subject, because I didn't want anyone overhearing.

The bell rang and we went in. As we walked through the swing doors to our classroom, Josh Adams tapped me on the shoulder.

'Megan, Miss Springer wants you,' he said. 'She said would you go to the staff room before your first lesson.'

Claire gasped theatrically. 'Oh, no!'

'Sshh!' I said.

'She must know!' said Claire in a stage whisper. 'D'you think she does?'

Naomi and a couple of the others were standing near us.

'Know what?' Naomi asked.

I glowered at Claire. 'Nothing!'

'Everyone will have to know soon,' Claire said under her breath, then she put her arm through mine. 'D'you want me to come with you?'

'No!' I said. I pulled my arm out from hers. 'Look,' I whispered urgently, 'Don't say anything to anyone – right?'

She shrugged. 'OK.'

'It might not even be that,' I said. 'It might be something completely different.'

I climbed the stairs to the staff room, feeling sick. Of course, I knew it *was* that. The doctor had said to Mum that the school would have to know straight away because of health and safety regulations, so either he or Mum must have phoned them. For two pins I'd have run off home, except I knew that Mum was there – she'd decided she had to take the whole day off to prepare for the social worker. And anyway, Miss Springer was all right; she was a bit soft but she wasn't scary.

When I put my head round the staff room door, every teacher there turned to look at me. I felt myself go red; it was obvious that they all knew. Knew and had been talking about me.

Miss Springer hurried over, looking flustered, her red hair awry. 'Wait for me outside, will you, Megan?'

When she came out she had a pile of papers in her arms. There was a bench outside the staff room and she sat down on this, nodding at me to do the same.

She coughed. 'Now, your mother has just telephoned,' she said. 'She said you might be . . . that is are . . .'

'Yeah, I'm having a baby,' I said, thinking that Mum might have told me that she was ringing.

'Yes, well . . . I've discussed it very briefly with Mr Tapson, and he agrees that we should try and keep you on at school as long as possible.'

I looked at her in surprise. I hadn't thought that I *wouldn't* stay on.

'You've got exams in June and it wouldn't be fair to exclude you from school at the moment.'

I nodded. Why should I be excluded anyway?

There was a long silence. Miss Springer touched my hand and asked kindly, 'How are you feeling, dear?'

A lump came into my throat. People had reacted so

differently: Claire had been amazed, Mum had been horrified and the doctor had been snotty. No one, up till now, had been kind or caring. Miss Springer was the first and it was a bit unexpected.

I sniffed, blinked and looked away.

'That's all right,' Miss Springer said. 'It's good to cry. It's no good bottling up your feelings at a time like this.'

'I don't want to cry . . . with everyone coming out . . . going into class,' I said, struggling. 'I don't want everyone to see.'

'Well, let's talk about practical matters instead, then,' she said. 'I understand it's too late for you to consider abortion and that the baby will be born in August.'

I nodded, looking at the floor.

'Is the father of the baby a boy from this school?'

Again I nodded.

'Are you still having a relationship with him?'

I shook my head.

'That's a pity. You're going to need lots of support and sometimes boys can be a pillar of strength. Have you told your friends at school?'

'Only one,' I said.

'Yes, well these things have a habit of getting out

very quickly, so it won't be long before everyone's tongues are wagging. Is that going to worry you?'

'I suppose so,' I said, shrugging. 'I don't really know.'

'Now, your mother sounded rather upset and shocked, and of course that's understandable. Do you usually have a close relationship with her, though?'

'Not really,' I said, biting my lip.

'That's a pity.' She smiled at me kindly. 'But I'm sure she'll come round in time.'

'She wants me to have the baby adopted!' I blurted out.

'And what do *you* want?'

I shook my head. 'I don't know.'

'Well, you've got a few months to think about it.' She looked down at the papers she held. 'Now, I've got some forms to fill in for the authorities, so I'm going to do that, see Mr Tapson again and speak to you soon.'

I nodded, grateful she was nice to me, pleased she seemed to be on my side. Miss Springer, I could see, felt useful. She'd come into her own. This was the sort of personal development she could get her teeth into.

I went back downstairs. Everyone was doing Art

81

by then, working on their GCSE projects in little groups.

Claire, who was working on a huge mural, beckoned me over. 'Was she all right? What did she say?' she asked in an excited whisper.

'I'll tell you at Break,' I said.

Claire nudged Josie, who was working next to her on the mural. 'I can't go with you over to the Sixth at Break,' she said. 'Megs and I have got something to talk about.'

'Oh yeah?' Josie said. 'What's so important that it'll keep you out of the Sixth?'

'Can't say,' Claire said. 'But it *is* very important.'

'Ooh-er!' Josie said, looking at us curiously.

I glowered at Claire. She was *dying* to tell people; absolutely *dying* to. 'I don't know why you don't put a bloody notice up,' I said under my breath.

She looked at me in pretend surprise. 'Don't be like that.'

'Well, you keep dropping hints all the time!'

'I don't!'

'Oh, OK. I'm imagining it, am I?'

She didn't say anything else then, but at lunchtime, when we were in the hall eating our sandwiches, she looked into my plastic box and said, 'You haven't got twice as much food, then?'

'What d'you mean?'

'Well, you know what they say . . . '

I looked at her blankly, not catching on, and she added in a whisper, 'You're supposed to be eating for *two* now, aren't you?'

I turned on her. 'Why d'you keep saying things like that?' I asked fiercely. 'Why don't you just shut up!'

'Sor-*ry*!' she said. 'I was just trying to cheer you up. Make a joke . . . you know?'

When I got home about two-fifteen I found Mum had practically redecorated the house ready for the social worker's visit. She'd waxed the sitting room floor, cleaned the windows and had even got the net curtains down, washed them and put them back.

'I'm exhausted,' she said, looking at me accusingly. 'Utterly exhausted.'

'I didn't ask you to do all that!' I said. This was the wrong thing to say, of course, and led to a tirade about me being responsible for the shame of having a social worker visit the house, and even if *I* didn't care what the house looked like when social workers came, *she* certainly did.

It all rolled over my head, really. At least it made a change from being frozen out.

At two-thirty Mum was standing by the window, muttering that it would be just like *them* if she was late. She also said that she hoped that the woman wasn't coming in uniform, or the neighbours would know already what we'd sunk to.

When the woman arrived five minutes later (not in uniform), the first thing Mum said as she ushered her into the sitting room was, 'I don't want you to think we're the sort of family who usually has social workers calling on them.'

I nearly died of embarrassment, but the woman just winked at me and said, 'Oh, we social workers don't mind who we call on.' Mum didn't know how to take this.

The woman was all right, actually. Her name was Susie and she was black and motherly and very matter-of-fact, acting as if she saw pregnant fifteen-year-olds every day of the week and not making me feel I should be walking round in sackcloth and ashes, continually apologising for my state.

She gave me lots of leaflets to read, filled in forms, and talked about antenatal visits and which hospital I would go to for the birth. She talked to me all the time, and when Mum tried to take over, always asked me what I thought. When Mum said she believed that adoption was the best, the only solution, Susie said it was too early to make those sort of decisions and we could talk over the options as the months went by. She said it would be the biggest decision I would ever make and I was to think carefully about what I wanted.

'What *you* want, mind,' she added, wagging a finger at me.

'Don't I have a say in what's best for my own daughter?' Mum interrupted.

'Of course you do, Mrs Warrell.'

'War*rell*,' Mum corrected.

'But ultimately, it will be Megan who has the final say.'

'How ridiculous! How can she know what's best at her age?'

'There's no one thing that's best,' Susie said calmly, 'but Megan must decide for herself what she wants to do. After all, it'll be her who has to live with that decision for the rest of her life.'

Mum made a *humph* noise. 'She should have thought of that.'

'Now, what about Megan's father?' Susie asked Mum. 'Will you be letting him know what's happened? Do you think he might help out financially?'

Mum tutted – and I realised with a jolt that I hadn't even thought of Dad.

'He's got a new family now,' Mum said. 'But he must certainly be told. I don't see why I should take the full brunt of it.' She sniffed. 'Though what good he'll do . . . ' her voice trailed off.

'And what about the father of your baby, Megan?' Susie asked me. 'Can you rely on him for any help? Is he able to shoulder some of the responsibility?'

I glanced nervously at Mum.

'Would you rather speak to me about this at some other time?' Susie asked.

I nodded and Mum's mouth went into a tight line.

'Of course,' Susie said. 'I've gone on quite enough for one day. I'll be visiting you every week from now on, so we'll have plenty of time to chat.'

'Every week!' Mum said. 'That's not necessary, surely.'

'I'm here to look after the welfare of your daughter and the welfare of your grandchild,' Susie said. Which shut Mum up.

When I showed Susie to the door she said, 'It's hard, I know, but from now on the whole system swings into operation and you'll have lots of people looking out for you. Your mum's had a terrible shock, but she'll come round. Mums nearly always do.'

I nodded and said thanks and goodbye. *Nearly always*. What was the betting that mine was the exception: the mother who *didn't* come round? What would happen then? What would happen to me and the baby?

When I went back into the sitting room, Mum was plumping up cushions.

'Two things,' she said sharply. 'Firstly, your sister will have to know. I'm going to tell her at the weekend.'

'All right,' I shrugged. Big deal, I thought.

'And I'm going to move her bed into my room for the time being. While you're . . . like you are. Until it's born.'

'What for?' I said. I didn't particularly like having Ellie in with me, I'd always wanted my own room, but Mum was speaking as if I had to be sectioned off; as if pregnancy was catching.

'I just don't happen to think it's appropriate for you to share a room with your ten-year-old sister,' she said. 'And that's all I'm saying on the matter.'

'OK,' I said.

'And the other thing is, I want you to think very seriously indeed about adoption, because there is NO

WAY that I'm having a baby in this house. Do you understand?'

I didn't reply. As if a baby would want to come and live with such an old crow as her anyway.

CHAPTER NINE

'**O**w!' I gave a little squeal of surprise. I'd felt something moving, I really had.

Lying flat on my back on my bed, I gingerly ran my fingers over my tummy, feeling the bumps and lumps under the skin. On Monday Susie had asked me if I'd felt the baby moving, and I'd said I hadn't without really thinking. But wondering about it later I'd realised that I'd felt strange jerks and bubbly movements for a while now, and not realised that they might have been the baby.

I stroked my tummy, and as I looked down at myself, I actually saw movement – a tiny lump – rise and then disappear.

'Oh, wow!' I whispered. One of the booklets Susie had given me said that at about six months – and I was nearly that now – you could not only feel movement, but actually pick out the location of the baby's arms and legs as they moved about in their small space.

I stared down again, but all was still. Had the baby

gone to sleep? It had been a funny sensation, feeling it moving about. It was thrilling, but at the same time it had made me feel slightly sick. Imagine having someone inside you. Like Alien . . .

I pulled my T-shirt down, sat up and reached under the bed for one of the pregnancy books. I had no need to hide it under a magazine, because it was Saturday morning and Ellie was right at that moment hearing what Mum called 'the shameful news'. When she came up, all would have been revealed.

I turned to the chapter headed 'Month by Month Changes' and read that at six months, as well as feeling distinct movement, the expectant mother would also notice stretch marks on her stomach, her bust and the tops of her legs.

Stretch marks . . . so that was what they were. I'd seen some horrible dark marks, like long narrow scars, on the tops of my legs, but I hadn't taken much notice of them. The book went on to say that rubbing oil into them might make them feel softer, but wouldn't eliminate them altogether. In other words, I'd always have stretch marks because of this baby, even if I lived to be a hundred. Oh, brilliant.

It said that the baby now measured from twenty-eight to thirty-six centimetres, which sounded huge and impossible to me – how was there room for all that baby? – but then I saw a drawing of it and remembered that it was curled right round with its knees almost to its chin. It still didn't look very nice, though, with its great big head and thick twirly cord attaching it to my insides.

I read a bit about protein and making sure the baby got enough nutrients, and then found a bit about breast feeding. *Absolutely* yuk. I just didn't like the thought of this funny little thing stuck on me, feeding off me like a leech. But then, if I was having it adopted, someone else would be feeding it anyway.

I tried to think about how that would feel, but I wasn't sure. I hadn't really known I was having a baby for long enough to think about what giving it up would be like. Only that it might be a relief. If I did, I could go back to being normal, being me again.

I stopped reading to go to the door and try and listen to what was going on in the kitchen. I couldn't hear a thing. They'd been ages. What on earth was Mum saying to her?

I flopped back on the bed and found something in the book about going to relaxation classes to help prepare for a good birth. I shivered. *Birth*. The only births I'd seen on TV were full of blood and gore with the woman screaming the place down. How did they stand it? How did they survive? Suppose I died of the pain? Why couldn't I go to sleep and have them just take it away?

I heard Ellie walking along the hall at last, but wasn't sure whether to face it out with her in a *So what* sort of way, or pretend I didn't know what they'd been talking about.

She came into the bedroom and I glanced up.

'It's okay, Mum's told me,' she said, and from her face it was obvious that she and Mum were together in their feelings on this: shock and disapproval were written all over her.

'Right,' I said.

'She's going to help me move all my stuff into her room this afternoon.'

'OK!' I said cheerfully. I wasn't going to let *her* make me feel guilty as well.

'Mum's crying down there,' she went on, looking at me accusingly. 'She's crying because she says none of the neighbours will talk to her once they know.'

'Don't be ridiculous. Who cares about them, anyway?'

'Mum does. But she says you'll probably have it adopted.'

'I don't know that yet! I haven't decided.'

'She says it can't come here – that there's no room for it here at all. And I don't want it here either.'

I didn't say anything.

'Girls aren't supposed to have babies before they get married,' she said in a priggy voice.

'No?' I said sarcastically. 'Well, aren't I the naughty one.'

'Mum's writing to Dad right now to tell him about you.'

'I thought you said she was crying?'

'She's going to ask him if you can go over there.'

'*What*?!'

'She says it will be best for you to go over there to have it and that he should have some of the . . .'

'Bloody cheek!' In a fury I rolled off the bed and charged down the hall.

Mum was in the kitchen, sitting at the table with a note-pad in front of her.

'Are you writing to Dad?' I demanded.

'Yes, I am,' she said, looking at me coldly. 'I don't see why I should have to bear all the worry of this. He can have you over there, see how he likes it.'

'I'm not a parcel!' I shouted, outraged. 'You can't send me off to the other side of the world just because you're worried what the neighbours will say. What about *me*? What about asking me if I want to go first?'

'Strikes me you've been given far too much of your own way,' she said. 'That's part of the reason you're in the state you're in.'

'Don't be stupid!' I said witheringly. 'It wasn't like that.'

'You're my daughter, you're underage, I can decide what's best for you,' she snapped. 'If I decide you'll go to Australia then that's where you'll go.'

'No, I won't! I'll run away, I . . . I'll get Susie to stop you. I don't want to go! I don't know anything about Australia and I don't know anything about Dad any more.' I paused for breath. 'Anyway, I'm not going and that's that!' I rushed at her, grabbed the pad and ran back to my bedroom.

Pushing past Ellie I threw myself on my bed and burst into tears. I hated Mum. I hated Ellie and I hated everyone. Why, just when I needed someone to be nice to me, were they all being so vile?

That afternoon Ellie and Mum moved all Ellie's stuff into the big bedroom. Neither of them asked me to help, and I didn't offer.

Good luck, I thought. Let them stew in there. So

what if they ganged up on me and I didn't have anyone?

When I thought that, tears came into my eyes, but then I had another thought: *I had the baby*. The baby was on my side. The baby was mine. I think this was the first good thought I'd ever had about it.

I went over to Claire's later and I started telling her about Ellie and everything, but though she listened she wasn't really taking it in. She had something else on her mind. Our holiday.

'You see, I'm not sure if we'll be going now,' she said, after a lot of humming and haaing.

'Why's that, then?'

'Well, I just said – because my dad doesn't know if he can get the time off work.'

'What, will we go a different week, then?'

'Dunno,' she said, looking embarrassed. 'One of my cousins has just been down there and apparently it wasn't very good. The swimming pool wasn't finished. Mum says we might have to cancel it altogether.'

'Oh,' I said.

'Well, you wouldn't have been able to go anyway, would you?' she said. 'You'll be *huge* in July.'

'I suppose not,' I said. July: I'd be eight months pregnant, big and lumbering and different.

I sighed, I didn't want to be different, and I didn't

want to be shut in a bedroom on my own and I didn't want to miss out on holidays. 'I might be able to go afterwards,' I said. 'At the end of August. Maybe your dad can get time off then.'

'What? And bring a baby on holiday with you?!' she said in alarm. 'What d'you think my mum and dad would say about that?'

'I meant that I could go on holiday if I had it adopted,' I said.

'I didn't think you wanted it adopted.'

'I might have to. Where would I live with a baby? My mum won't have it living at home,' I said bitterly. 'She's trying to get rid of *me* in Australia.'

'Can't you get a flat or something?'

'On my own? I don't want to live on my own.'

'You wouldn't be, would you? You'd have a little baby.'

I shrugged. It was no use trying to imagine it because I just *couldn't*.

'So, shall we say the holiday's off?' she asked after a moment. 'Be easier, wouldn't it? Save us being disappointed later.'

'OK,' I said slowly.

'Sorry and all that. My dad couldn't help it, though. 'Spect we'll go another year.'

We did a bit of homework. Part of our GCSEs were marked on coursework, but we had the first of our actual sit-down exams in a few weeks' time and everyone was getting down to revision.

A bit later the phone rang and Claire's mum called that it was Josie.

Claire went into the hall and when her mum was handing over the phone I heard her say in a low voice, 'Did you say anything?' and Claire said, 'Sssh! Yes.'

I stayed at the door, listening. Claire had sworn that she hadn't told her mum I was expecting, but what if she had, and her mum had said that I couldn't go on holiday with them?

Claire was speaking to Josie very quietly. 'Yes, she's here now. No, I can't do that! Don't be silly. Yeah, I'll let you know.'

My cheeks burned. She'd told her! She'd told Josie.

She put the phone down and came in again. 'Josie wanted to know which bit of English coursework we've got to give in first.'

I stared at her. 'You've told her, haven't you?'

'No!'

'You have. I know you have. She didn't ring to ask you anything about coursework.'

Claire gave a great big sigh. 'Oh, all right – she

does know. It doesn't really matter, though, does it? They'd have had to know soon enough.'

'*They?!*'

'I went round to Josie's house last night and Naomi was there,' she said moodily.

I was silent, trying to take this in. We *never* did things like going to people's houses without each other.

'Josie rang me after school and she asked you to go over as well,' Claire said, 'but I said I didn't think you'd go because you weren't feeling very well. You weren't!' she added defensively. 'You keep not feeling well.'

'All right, let me guess,' I said. 'You went round there and they asked *why* wasn't I feeling well, and you told them.'

'I didn't!' she said. 'Not just like that. Not for ages. They thought of it themselves in the end.'

'I expect they did,' I said bitterly. 'What did you do – stuff a pillow up your jumper and give them three guesses?'

'Don't be daft. It wasn't at all like that.'

'So how many people know now?'

'Only those two. And they've promised faithfully not to tell anyone else.'

'Oh, no,' I said. 'Of course they won't!' I glowered at her. 'I thought I could trust you. I thought you were my best friend!'

'I am! Oh, sorry, Megs, I just . . . '

I didn't want to hear the rest. I got up, grabbed my homework and went out, slamming her door and their front door behind me. Then I cried all the way home.

CHAPTER 10

The following Monday morning I was alone in the flat. Mum and Ellie had gone off to work and school, but as Susie was coming to see me again at 9.30, I had to stay behind and miss the first two lessons. Missing lessons, come to think of it, was just about the only good thing that had come out of being pregnant.

I'd got dressed and was sitting at the kitchen table drinking tea, wondering what was going to happen to me. I was having a daydream in which Mum was one of those lovely mums you see in advertisements, supportive and doting and sympathetic, and Ellie was a keen younger sister, doing things for me and excited about the coming baby. Luke and I weren't going out together, but he was standing by ready to visit me in hospital and buy the baby a pram, and Claire and the rest of my friends were a solid bunch behind me, ready to attack if anyone said anything nasty.

None of this was true, though. *None of it.* It seemed

to me that I had no one on my side: Mum wanted to ship me off to Australia, Ellie thought I was some species of low life, Luke wasn't interested and my best friend was having a great time telling everyone my secrets.

I heaved a big sigh. I hated every part of my life; hated being pregnant. It was ridiculous; how could so much trouble, so many consequences, come from such a tiny little incident as that had been? It really hadn't been so important a thing to have caused such an avalanche of happenings.

Susie's green Mini drew up outside the flats. *She* was on my side, I thought. Then I remembered that she was a professional, paid to be on my side.

She was nice, though. I was glad I had her.

'How have you been then, ducks?' she asked. She put her arm round me as I poured her a cup of tea and I only just managed to stop myself from crying again.

'Normal!' she said, looking at my face as I sniffed back tears of self-pity. 'You've been normal. You know what they say, don't you: *Three months dreary, three months cheery, three months weary . . .* '

'I missed the three months dreary,' I said, 'and practically missed the three months cheery – and what I had of it wasn't exactly cheery anyway.'

'So you're into three months weary,' Susie said. 'That just means you'll be tired a lot of the time.'

'Oh, great.'

'Keep taking those vitamins and iron, won't you? How are you getting on at school? Were they all right about it?'

I nodded. 'Miss Springer was nice, and none of the other teachers has really said anything. On Friday night, though, my so-called best friend told a couple of our other friends, so I don't think it'll be long before everyone and his auntie finds out.'

'How has your mum been?'

I pulled a face. 'A nightmare,' I said. 'She's still freezing me out, and she's told my sister now. They've ganged up against me.'

'Now, I'm sure that's not true!' she said.

'It is. Mum won't let Ellie and me share a bedroom anymore. She thinks I'm an evil influence.'

'*I* think it's a very good idea for you to have a bedroom of your own. You need some privacy. You don't want your sister goggling at you every time you get undressed. I think your mum realises that.'

'It's not that,' I mumbled. 'She thinks I'll lead Ellie astray.'

She shook her head and, putting her mug down,

got a pink card out of her bag. 'Now, I've got your first hospital appointment through and it's vital that you go; you've missed a couple already because of finding out so late. It's for next Tuesday, so if your mum can't have the time off to go with you, maybe you've got an aunt or gran or someone living nearby . . .'

I shook my head. 'We've only got Auntie Lorna, Dad's sister,' I said, 'and she's miles away. She doesn't even know I'm expecting yet.'

'Well, I might be able to come to the hospital with you myself,' Susie said. 'Speaking of your dad – does he know yet?'

I shook my head. 'Mum started writing to him at the weekend – she was asking him if I could go over there and have the baby – she wanted to get rid of me! I stopped her, though, and now she says I've got to write and tell him myself.'

'Well, I suggest you do that,' Susie said. 'If he's prepared to help you out financially it would be nice to know about it as soon as possible.'

'I don't know if he will,' I said. 'He's got other children now.'

'Well, write and see.'

We talked about other things: feelings, mostly, and a bit about adoption and what it would entail. I said I still couldn't decide and she said if I did want to keep the baby, there would be people to help me. I asked if I'd be able to get a flat and she said not straight away, and that if Mum still wouldn't let me come home with the baby I might have to go in bed and breakfast accommodation. She gave me another book to read, and said I should go to childbirth classes to do exercises.

I shook my head. 'Can't I do them at home? I don't want to go to a class. They'll all look at me.'

'Of course they won't!' she said briskly, taking her mug to the sink.

'They'll all have husbands with them. They'll be normal.'

'Huh!' she said. 'What's normal?'

She went off and I got ready for school. The only way I could get my school skirt on now was to have the zip undone all the way down with an elastic band through the buttonhole and over the button, pulling the waistband together. I had to wear my shirt outside my skirt to hide this, and the shirt was straining across my bust, pulling and gaping between the buttons. All in all, I wasn't stunning.

I looked at myself in the mirror, pulling a comb through my greasy hair. I looked fat and frumpy. *And* spotty. Funny that it said in one of the pregnancy books that women looked at their most beautiful during pregnancy. They were radiant; they *bloomed*.

I turned away from the mirror. I didn't want to go to school. It was partly because I couldn't think about ordinary things like lessons and exams when my mind was full up with BABY and partly because of Claire. I was still angry with her, and wondering exactly what she'd said to Josie and Naomi and what they'd said back. I knew it was crazy me worrying about them when I scoffed at Mum being worried about the neighbours, but I just was.

By the time I'd got to school, though, I'd remembered Susie saying how important it was to be positive, and given myself a talking to. After all, I'd had rows with Claire before and we'd always got over them. And people like Josie and Naomi wouldn't turn against me just because I was having a baby. I was still the same person.

I'd missed two lessons so it was Break when I got there, and drizzling a bit so there was hardly anyone in the playground, only a few boys from our class kicking a ball around. One of them looked at me and shouted, 'Wah-hey!' and the others snorted with laughter, but I didn't think anything of it.

When I got in to our tutor room, though, there was a group of about ten girls sitting on a table, talking intently.

As I went in, Vinny looked round, saw me and hissed, 'Ssh! Here she is!'

It was like when I'd gone into the staff room: every single person in there looked round at me. I felt myself go scarlet and nearly turned and ran out, but something made me carry on walking. I put my bag down. 'OK, then,' I said, my voice all wobbly. 'Everyone knows, do they?'

Claire got up and came over to me. 'Sorry,' she said, 'but it wasn't my fault. Miss Springer came in looking for you this morning and then Vinny guessed, and told Josie what she thought and . . . it just got round.'

'Is it really true?' April said.

'Is it Luke's?' one of the boys asked.

'How far gone are you?' said another.

There was a shout of, 'Didn't think you had it in you!' and someone said, 'She did have!' and everyone roared with laughter.

I fought hard not to start crying.

'Would have tried it on myself if I'd known!' a boy called.

'D'you give it out to everyone?' said another.

'Here, would you do me a turn for a quid?'

There was another roar of laughter and calls of, 'What a slapper!' and 'Bet she's a right goer!' and I *did* start crying then.

Claire came over and put her arm round me. 'Leave her alone, will you?' she said angrily to the boys.

I couldn't take any more, though. I shrugged Claire off, ran out of the class and spent all the next lesson hiding in the lavatories, crying.

I thought about going home, but then had some notion about facing it out. Perhaps once I'd stood up to everyone and let them get over it, then it would be all right. They'd *have* to get over it, otherwise I couldn't stay on at school and do my exams.

I found Claire at lunchtime and we went into the dinner hall together, but news about me must have spread like a tidal wave throughout the school, because people were nudging each other, looking me up and down and sniggering wherever I went.

I didn't know what it was like for Luke safe in the Sixth Form block, but I'm sure it can't have been anywhere near as bad. He wasn't any different; it wasn't him who was walking around with an elastic band holding his clothes together and a lump sticking out in front of him.

Claire was quite good, actually, because she was acting like a minder, grabbing my arm and helping me through squashes of people and vetting questions when anyone asked anything too stupid. I was glad she was around.

'It's all right,' she said, 'It's just a five minute wonder. Once everyone gets used to the idea . . . '

But when we had double Art that afternoon every member of every class that came by the art room looked through the window at me, and some banged on the door, and once I heard four or five of them go by singing something with the word Baby in the title. In class, too, everything that was said – every single thing – had some double meaning which caused roars of laughter.

It was terrible. If I'd had a shell I would have crept into it and hidden.

That wasn't the very worst bit, though. At home time Claire and I went to get our stuff from our lockers, with people staring at me all the way and jostling each other to get a good view.

I made the mistake of shouting at them: 'I haven't got two heads, you know!' which caused someone to shout back, 'No, you've got a bun in the oven!' and everyone shrieked.

Claire and I got our jackets and crossed the playground together. At the school gates were about seven boys from the year below us. They fell silent as we came up to them, then as I walked by, began a chant: 'Ea-zee meat . . . ea-zee meat . . . ea-zee meat'.

I clutched at Claire's arm.

'Don't take any notice!' she said, pulling me on.

'Slag!' one of them shouted. 'She's anyone's!'

'Anyone's! Anyone's!' the others yelled, and then the *Ea-zee meat . . . ea-zee meat!* started again.

I turned on them. 'I'm not! I'm not!' I screamed, and then I burst into tears, dropped my bag and ran all the way home.

CHAPTER 11

I stayed in my bedroom until Mum came in from work, and I wouldn't have come out then but she yelled at me to go down to the kitchen *immediately*.

'Listen to this,' she said, nodding at Ellie. 'Go on,' she encouraged her. 'Say it again.'

'There's boys outside the flats,' Ellie said dutifully. 'A crowd of boys. They shouted at me.'

'And what did they say?' Mum asked, tight-lipped. She was still wearing one of her office suits: neat, navy-blue, with a pleated skirt and horrible frilly blouse. She looked like a member of the royal family opening a hospital.

'They said, 'Your sister's up the duff.' What's that mean, up the duff?'

'It means,' Mum said slowly, 'that your sister is having a baby.'

'As you very well know,' I said to Ellie bitterly.

Mum turned on me. 'And what have you got to say for yourself?'

I shrugged. 'Nothing,' I muttered. 'What d'you expect me to say?'

'Everyone knows about you now, I take it?'

'Some girls at school found out,' I said.

'I should say they did. That was your best friend, I suppose? Never have trusted that girl.'

I turned away.

'Just a minute,' she said. 'You and I are going out.'

I looked at her. 'Where to?'

'That boy's house.'

I felt my stomach lurch. 'What?'

'To see his parents.'

'We *can't*!'

'Oh, yes we can. I'm not having this . . . this trouble brought on our home. He's got to be made to share the responsibility.'

I felt faint. Imagine going round to Luke's house . . . accusing him . . . having a row . . . Mum shouting and screaming. Suppose he hadn't told his mum and dad yet? Suppose he said it wasn't his?

'We can't!' I said again. But I knew that Mum, in one of these sorts of moods, was unstoppable.

'Yes, we can,' she snapped. 'I'm not having all this – gangs hanging about outside the house, Ellie frightened to go out, you making an exhibition of yourself.

112

His family are going to have to take some of the burden. They'll have to pay for you to go away somewhere.'

'I don't want to go away somewhere! Anyway, it was just a few boys shouting,' I said, glad that Ellie was still at primary school, so hadn't witnessed what had gone on at *my* school that day. How was I ever going to go back again? Maybe, I thought, I did want to go away somewhere . . .

'The entire neighbourhood must know!' Mum went on.

'So who cares? Why don't we just pretend that we're not bothered, that we're taking it in our stride.'

'*What?*'

'It's only because you're so worried about what people think that they'll be talking. If you didn't put on airs and graces all the time and try to pretend you're something you're not, then . . . '

'How dare you!' she said. 'I've worked non-stop to maintain standards; I've brought up you and your sister single-handed. I taught you to read before you went to school; you were the only children round here to go to ballet lessons! I thought I'd taught you right from wrong – but you've let me down disgracefully.'

'Oh go on, then, chuck me out!' I said. 'You've

been trying to get rid of me ever since I told you. Perhaps you'd like me to go and live in a cardboard box somewhere.'

'I've worked my fingers to the bone for you and this is how you've repaid me!'

I gave a bitter sort of sigh. This was the old *After all I've done for you* speech I'd heard so many times before, dressed in new clothes with an extra spadeful of emotional blackmail thrown in. 'It wasn't my fault,' I muttered.

'Then whose fault was it?' she demanded.

I was silent. It was Luke's fault, I supposed, for telling me it would be all right and I couldn't possibly get pregnant. But then again it was my fault because I shouldn't have believed him. It was my body, so the final responsibility was mine; it was me who would have to suffer – was suffering – now.

'Get your coat on. Something long. Something to hide the state of you,' Mum said, looking at me in disgust. She went along the hall to her bedroom.

'Is Luke the father of the baby?' Ellie asked. 'Are you really going round there?'

I didn't reply. Again I wished I could run away, but knew it would do no good. I'd still be pregnant however far I ran.

I did think of taking Mum somewhere completely different, and end up knocking at the front door of a stranger, but she'd already looked up Luke's name in the phone book and naturally, because of working in an estate agent's, knew exactly where he lived.

I'd been round to his house and met his mum and dad before, when I'd been going out with him. He lived in a really nice house, close to the park, with five bedrooms because there were three children and his dad worked at home.

'They've got money, then,' Mum said sniffily, looking up at the house.

I was silent, feeling sick and shaky.

'I'm surprised we haven't heard from them before, frankly. Looking at this house you'd think they know how to behave. Least they could have done would have been to contact me and offer their apologies; asked what they could do to help.'

'I don't know if Luke's even told them,' I said.

'It'll be a nice surprise, then. About time they knew what their son's been up to.' We went up the steps and she looked appraisingly at the newly painted door with its shiny brass letterbox and handle. 'Oh, they're doing very nicely thank you, aren't they? While thanks to what their son has done, my house is under siege from gangs.'

Honestly, I could have laughed if it hadn't been so pathetic. So ludicrous. If the whole thing hadn't been such a misery.

Mum rang the bell. There was one slight chance, one hope I had: that everyone was out.

But they weren't.

Luke opened the door. He saw me and his face went pale.

'Are your parents in?' Mum asked frostily.

Luke stared at her. I could see that he wanted to say no – but Rosie, his little sister, had pushed herself between him and the door and was looking at us curiously.

'Dad's upstairs,' Rosie said.

'Well, Luke, would you tell him we're here? I suppose you know what it's about.'

Luke half closed the door and disappeared.

Mum sniffed. 'We're not even given the courtesy of being invited in.'

I hugged my arms around myself, feeling wretched. Luke's face . . . he'd looked at me as if I'd betrayed him, given him away. What else could I have done, though? And besides, although I didn't want to go about it *this* way, wasn't Mum right, shouldn't he and his family do something to help?

He was ages and ages, so that in the end Mum rang the doorbell again. Rosie was sitting on the stairs, staring at us all the time. And still no one came.

Eventually Mum rang the bell for the third time. 'I'm going in,' she said determinedly. 'I can't wait out here all day. What do they think I am: a door-to-door salesman?'

To my horror she pushed open the front door and shouted up the stairs. 'Is anyone home? Mr Compton?'

'Who's that?' a man's voice answered.

I leaned against the doorframe, feeling weak.

'Come *in*!' Mum hissed at me. 'Don't just stand there.'

'We can't . . . '

Luke's dad came down the stairs, looking confused. 'What's going on? I heard someone ringing the door and then looked out and saw Luke disappearing down the garden.'

'Hah!' Mum said scornfully. 'Well, he would, wouldn't he?'

It was a farce. I wanted to scream and laugh at the same time.

Luke's dad looked at me. He wasn't a bit like Luke, he was shortish and bald, with a round face. 'It's

Megan, isn't it? What are you . . .'

'Your son hasn't told you yet, then?' Mum said.

'Told me what?' he asked warily.

'Told you that he's got my daughter pregnant.'

Mr Compton's face whitened, then became hard and set, like a mask. 'Who says?'

'Who says? She does, of course. She's six months pregnant and your son is the father.'

There was a long silence while I squirmed and Luke's dad took this in, then he said, 'I'm afraid I can't possibly comment on this at the moment.'

'What d'you mean?' Mum said. 'I don't want you to comment on it, I just want some help. Practical help.'

'I must speak to Luke, and Luke's mother, and then we'll contact you.' He opened the front door wider. 'You'll be hearing from us.'

'Oh, no you don't!' Mum said. 'You're not fobbing me off like that.'

'I'm sorry,' he said, 'I've got absolutely no proof that this is my son's child – and I must say I rather doubt it. Until I've spoken to Luke I'm not saying another word. Goodbye,' he added pointedly.

I was halfway down the path at this, but Mum wasn't so easily got rid of.

'Are you implying that my daughter is *lying*?'

'I'm not implying anything,' he said, 'and I'm not admitting anything, either. Goodbye,' he said again.

He'd half-closed the door by this time so Mum had no option but to step back. 'We're coming back tomorrow,' she said. 'I want something sorted out. I want Luke to take responsibility for what he's done.'

The door closed on us. The last thing I heard was Rosie asking, 'Is Megan having a baby?'

On the way home I decided that it had to be the worst day ever, worse than the day I'd found out about the baby, worse than the day I'd told Mum. When we got home, though, I discovered that things could get even more awful.

'The phone's been ringing all the time,' Ellie said. She wasn't allowed to answer the phone or the door if she was on her own. 'Ringing and ringing.'

Mum did 1471. It was a local number, but not one that we knew. I was just about to slink off to my room and think about things – mostly what it was going to be like at school the next day and how I could get out of going – when it began ringing again.

'Wait!' Mum said to me.

She picked up the phone. 'Yes,' I heard her say, and then just, 'I see. Quite. What about her own exams? Yes, I understand.'

There were a few more tight, clipped words, and then she put the phone down. 'That was Mr Tapson, your head teacher,' she said to me.

I stared at her.

'Apparently there was a lot of fuss and disruption today, and it all centred on you. Is that right?'

I nodded. 'Yes, but I didn't start it. It wasn't . . . '

'Mr Tapson rang to say that he has decided, in everyone's best interests, that you should be excluded from school from now on. He said he can't allow pupils who're taking exams to be disturbed. What d'you think of that, young lady?'

'What?' I said incredulously. 'It wasn't my fault everyone made a stupid fuss!'

'No,' Mum snapped. 'It never is your fault, is it?'

'What did he mean? What about my exams and everything?'

'He meant just that – you're excluded from school. You've been expelled!'

CHAPTER 12

~ Letters from Megan ~

Train somewhere between Portsmouth and Chester

Wednesday, May 10th

Dear Claire,

I didn't have time to ring you or come round, and anyway, since Monday Mum's been standing over me breathing fire, watching my every move. I was glad to get away in the end because every time I said anything, or did anything, it made her worse. She was in total bitch phase.

Of course you've heard by now that I was expelled from school. Well, they call it being excluded, but it's the same thing: they don't want me there. Tappy told

Mum that I was a disruptive influence. *Me!*

What happened was, after Monday and all the fuss, Tappy phoned Mum to say that they couldn't have me at school any more. She went MAD at me (this was after a trip round to Luke's house with her – tell you later). She rang up Susie, my social worker, and *she* came round and calmed everything down and began trying to find 'an alternative arrangement'. This turned out to be staying with my Auntie Lorna in Chester, and I'm on my way there now. While I'm with her I'm going to a special school for pregnant mums where I can take my GCSEs, which stopped Mum going quite so mad. I think it'll be all right at Auntie Lorna's – better than at home, anyway. Mum was a thing demented.

Anyway, when I didn't turn up at school, what did everyone say? Were you told what had happened to me officially?

I went to the hospital yesterday for my first antenatal appointment. They had to bring it forward specially. Susie came with me, and the nurses filled in forms and the doctor examined me (another internal – yuk) and everything was all right except they said that my pelvis was rather small, so they don't want me to have a baby that's too huge or I might not get it out! I had a scan and am booked there, in St Bride's, to have the baby. I'll be back from Auntie Lorna's in time for that.

I still can't really believe that I'm having a *baby*. When I wake up in the mornings I nearly always think I've dreamed it (nightmared it). I think I probably will have it adopted, I can't see how I could manage otherwise. Susie said I don't *have* to, and that if I kept it (Mum will never let me have it at home), eventually I'd get a flat. First I'd have to go into Bed and Breakfast, though, and I don't fancy that. They're awful, those places, I've seen them on TV. You have to walk round the streets all day because they won't let you stay in your room.

Anyway, after I'd been to hospital I went home and packed my stuff and Susie did a lot of phoning. She's transferring me to a social worker in Chester who'll look after me while I'm here.

All my coursework from school is being sent to this special school. I think it'll be really weird to just be with girls who are pregnant. It was a nightmare at our school on Monday, wasn't it? I felt like a criminal or something. It's a bit of a relief, really, that Tappy expelled me because I don't know how I'd ever have faced going back. I don't reckon it's fair: we know lots of girls who've slept with their boyfriends – some with more than one – who haven't got caught. But just because I have, they're calling me a slag. Well, what are they, then?

Luke: it was a nightmare. Mum insisted on going round to his house and I couldn't talk her out of it. He answered the door, and then just disappeared, and when his dad eventually appeared, *he* said what proof did we have that it was Luke's baby and other horrible things like that. Mum said she was going to go back there again the next day, but then all this happened, so at least I've been saved that.

I hope my Auntie Lorna will be all right. I can remember her from when she used to live near us and she was always nice then; she used to come and take me out for days. She takes photographs for a living, for magazines and so on. Mum says I'll be in the way there (but she would say that).

Will you write and tell me what's going on? What are people saying about me? Have you seen Luke?

Love from Megan

PS: My address is 12 Armitage Close, Chester.

12 Armitage Close,
Chester

May 11th

Dear Mum,

Just a note to say I am settling in okay. Lorna (she's told me to call her that and not Auntie) says she rang you last night to say I'd arrived safely.

She is very nice, and doesn't make me feel that I'm in the way at all. I think she looks a bit like that photo of Dad I've got. She's quite tall, with long black hair and slanting eyes. She's made her spare room into a bedroom for me and it's got some of her photographs on the walls. They're amazing!

I expect it is quiet there without me. Just how you like it! I'll be writing to Dad at the weekend. I don't know whether I'll get round to asking him for money, though.

Love from Megan

12 Armitage Close,
Chester

May 14th

Dear Dad,

Bet you're surprised to get a letter from me at this address.

A lot has happened. Firstly I have to tell you that I'm having a baby. I'm sorry if it's a terrible shock (it was to me, too). I am up here because it all got a bit hairy at home – you know what Mum's like – and then I was excluded from school. I didn't mind being excluded in the end because everyone was really awful to me. Anyway, I've got a social worker and she found out that there's a special educational unit near Auntie Lorna's so I've been sent here to go to that, to do my GCSEs and generally chill out a bit.

I like Lorna (she says I've got to call her that). She's really interesting, she treats me like a grown up and she tells me stories about when you were both little. I wish I'd known my gran (your mum, I mean). I expect you know that Mum's mum died two years ago.

Well, I hope this hasn't been too much of a shock

to you. Mum went completely bananas when I told her about the baby, so I'm quite glad that I didn't have to tell you face to face. I expect you want to know about the father of my baby. Well, it's a boy called Luke that I was going out with for a while around last Christmas. He was okay and I thought I loved him at the time, but we split up shortly after I got pregnant (although I didn't know I was at the time). I didn't find out I was pregnant until early April and I'm about six months now, so it's not long to go. Mum is dead set for me to have the baby adopted so I expect that's what I'll do. I'll be able to get back to normal, then. Although some babies are nice, I'm not sure that I feel grown up enough to bring one up all on my own. And there's the cost of it as well.

I am eating healthily and all that. I wonder if I'll ever see you again? Mum was going to write to you and demand that you have me over there, baby and all! I made her stop, though. I'd like to see you one day but I don't feel like travelling at the moment. Chester is far enough. It's funny to think I've got two half-sisters that I've never met. I wonder if they're like Ellie?! She and I don't get on brilliantly at the moment. I think she's at a funny age, but Mum says that it's *me* who's at the funny age.

I'm feeling quite tired tonight so I'm going to bed early. I'm on my own a lot in the evenings because Lorna goes off into her dark room to develop photographs, but I don't mind that.

I know I haven't always replied to your letters before, but I'd really like it if you wrote to me now.

Lots of love, Megan

12 Armitage Close,
Chester

17th May

Dear Susie,

I promised to write and let you know how I was getting on.

Lorna has made me feel really at home; we get on great. She's dead clever and takes fantastic photographs of gardens and houses. She gets commissions from magazines; it's a brilliant job.

I've met my new social worker, her name is Cathy and she seems really nice (not as nice as you, of course). She took me along to Cottesloe, the educational unit, last week and introduced me round. Hopefully all my coursework from school will have arrived there now, ready for the exams.

Cottesloe: it was GREAT. I didn't realise that there would be girls there who'd had their babies, as well as pregnant ones. In fact, most of them have already had them, so the babies are being looked after in the nursery while the girls study or take exams. There are five quite small babies, three toddlers, and also a little boy who is nearly three. His mum had him when she was 12!

The unit is in a big portable office place. Half of it is a nursery and the rest is made into rooms (kitchen, rest room, offices, etc). The ladies who look after the babies are really lovely, and so are the teachers. Everyone is allowed to play with the babies and they also have classes to teach you to care for them, bath them and stuff like that. I don't think that will concern me too much as I'll probably have the baby adopted. I *think* I will. The thing is, no one else here is having their baby adopted. Cathy says part of the reason for this is that housing isn't so critical here as where we live, so there are more flats for single girls.

I've made friends with a girl called Amy whose baby is due about the same time as mine. She has a boyfriend, though, AND a mum and dad who have agreed that she can go back home with the baby. I tell her she doesn't know how lucky she is. I think I might feel differently about adoption if Mum said that I could take the baby back home to live. But then I would still have a baby to take care of FOR EVER. I don't know if I want that.

I'm feeling quite tired lately (three months weary?) and my back aches quite a bit. I'm glad to be up here, though, where no one knows me. I feel quite normal at Cottesloe.

Hope to hear from you. Cathy said she is e-mailing you with some info you wanted about me. I go to the hospital for ante-natal next week and I am registered with Lorna's doctor as a temporary resident, so all that is taken care of. Thank you for sorting things out and getting me moved up here.

Lots of love, Megan

12 Armitage Close,
Chester

19th May

Dear Miss Springer,

Just a note to thank you for sending all the coursework for my GCSEs. It arrived on Monday at Cottesloe, the educational unit, and Janine there (it's all first names), who is the head, has arranged for me to take my exams with the others. She said that some of the coursework will be different, also one or two of the set texts, but I'm just going to concentrate on the ones we studied and they're going to put a note on my papers to explain. I've been doing quite a bit of reading to try and catch up, so I hope I don't do too badly. Who knows, I may be back at school with you next September starting A levels!

I'm getting on all right, just tired a lot of the time. Lorna (my auntie) is top notch, though. She's a career woman and has never married, so Mum thought I might be in the way, but Lorna says that it's a real treat to have me around the place.

Thanks for being very nice to me at school. I will

let you know what I have and try and write after the exams. Please remember me to anyone who asks about me (teachers, I mean).

Love from Megan

12 Armitage Road,
Chester

26th May

Dear Claire,

Thanks for your letter, it was great to hear from you, although it made me feel a bit homesick and strange reading about Jo's birthday party and you all going round to Vinny's to watch a video and all that stuff with ME NOT THERE! It feels years ago that I was part of all that. I can't imagine having nothing else to worry about except for having your hair go right or having the right trainers.

Thanks also for the Best Hairstyles Top Ten. I don't agree with number six, other than that they are OK.

I nearly rang you last night when I got your letter, but Lorna's phone is in the kitchen and she can hear everything (not that that matters as she is really ace), and I don't like to use it too much because of the cost.

Anyway, is everyone still gossiping about me? Sounds as if you are doing all right as my spokeswoman! Perhaps you ought to do a press conference and answer everyone's questions at the same time.

That dress you've bought sounds pretty good. I wish I could get into something that wasn't a sack. I'm quite glad you can't see me because I look ENOR-MOUS now, and will get ENORMOUSER. I'm about seven months. I went to the hospital yesterday and they said I was 'big for my dates', whatever that means. Fat, I think.

Have you seen Luke again? I think it's a bit off that he hasn't done anything to get in touch with me. I mean, I know I'm not at home, but he could find out where I am if he wanted to. Anyway, it's a good job I've gone off him because he'd never fancy me now: apart from being fat I've got stretch marks every-where and my hair is a total disaster. Enough comes out when I brush it to stuff a cushion with.

Art exam at the end of this week. I'll be taking it at the same time as you, so think of me, won't you?

Write again, lots of love from Megan

12 Armitage Road,
Chester

30th May

Dear Dad,

Thanks for your letter. I think your writing was OK, even though you say you were so shocked that your hand was shaking. I'm sure you're not ready to be a grandad – I'm not ready to be a mum, either!

I'm getting on brilliantly at Lorna's, we have lots of talks and quite a few laughs. I couldn't understand why she hasn't got married (she's *so* lovely) but when I asked her she said she'd had offers, but not the offer she wanted. Big heartbreak hinted at – was that when you were both teenagers? Do you remember who it was?

At weekends she sometimes takes me out with her on jobs or we just go looking for interesting places for her to photograph. She's started telling me a bit about shutter speeds and lenses and so on, and last night I helped her develop some photos. I get on better with her than with Mum, to tell you the truth, though the funny thing is, I'm missing Mum and Ellie a bit. I think about my old life at home (pre-pregnancy, I mean) and it all seems utterly blissful. I can't think what I ever had to moan about.

Thanks for saying you're going to send me some baby clothes. Not being funny but I'd rather have the money for a few maternity things now, because I don't know if I'm going to keep the baby. I keep changing my mind according to who I speak to. The girls at my new school are all keeping theirs, but most of them have got support from their families and I know I won't get that from Mum. She just wants me to have the baby, give it away and forget all about it.

Thanks for sending me the photos of Beth and Janine. It was nice to see them; I don't think they look at all like me or Ellie. You said you'd invite me out there to live with you except there isn't the room. That's OK, I wouldn't lumber you and Joyce with me and a baby. Or even me on my own.

I'll write again soon. I can't seem to concentrate on TV and it makes a change from reading my set books.

Lots of love, Megan

27 Armitage Road,
Chester

June 1st

Dear Mum,

It was nice to get a letter from you. I haven't written back before because I've been studying as much as I can. Fancy you thinking it's too quiet at home without me. I thought you'd love it!

I've taken quite a few exams now; just got two History papers at the end of the week and an RI one next week and that's the lot. I really don't know how I've done. All the questions were a nightmare when I first looked at them, but I managed to find something to say when I actually got started.

You don't have to worry about me being a nuisance to Lorna. I help her with meals (actually cooked spag. bol. all on my own last night) and do my own washing and ironing and so on.

You asked me if I'd thought any more about what I'm going to do when I've had the baby. The answer to that is: *I don't think of anything else.* I think I've got it all straight in my head, that I'll have mine adopted, and then I see the babies belonging to the girls in the unit, all cuddly and soft and gorgeous, and go all flakey about it.

I don't know why you've told Mrs Crimmon down the road that I've gone away because I've got bad asthma. She'll find out and then we'll both look stupid. I wish you wouldn't make things up, Mum. I know you do it because you don't want people talking about us, but when they find out the truth they'll just talk even more.

I had another antenatal appointment at the hospital, also another scan. I've seen the baby on a monitor now, and the woman in charge said she could see what sex it was, but I wouldn't let her tell me. One part of me wants to know and the other part doesn't. If it's being adopted then it doesn't matter either way, does it?

Love from Megan

PS: I've enclosed a letter for Ellie.

Dear Ellie,

Thanks for your letter and paintings. I've put the one of the blue flowers up on the wall. Lorna says it shows real creativity and you should think about going to art school!

I'm getting on all right. You should see the babies at school with me! You'd love them. At lunchtimes, all the girls who are still expecting rush into the nursery to pick up the babies and help feed them. Their real mums don't mind, they're glad of the break.

See you quite soon! Only a couple of weeks and I'll be home.

Love from Megan

12 Armitage Road,
Chester

June 6th

Dear Luke,

I was surprised to hear from you. You say you asked Claire for my address last Monday. Funnily enough, that was just after I'd written to her complaining that you'd blanked me out. Was this just a coincidence, or did she come and see you to persuade you to write?!

I hope your mum and dad didn't give you too hard a time after we left. Your dad seemed quite stern and scary. I'm sorry we just turned up on the doorstep like that; I'd have rung to warn you if I'd had the chance, but Mum suddenly got a bee in her bonnet and off we went. I think she's calmed down a bit since I've been up here, in fact I've just had a letter from her saying she's missing me. Can hardly believe this, considering we were always rowing, but in a funny way I've been missing her, too.

I'm not missing much else at home. My last day at school was a complete nightmare. I expect you've heard about it.

I'm glad your A levels are going well. I don't know

how I'll do in my exams, I still feel a bit woolly-headed and don't think of much else but being pregnant. If the exams all go wrong, I suppose I'll just have to do retakes.

I don't know what I'm doing about the baby: keeping it/not keeping it. I still can't decide. I think I'll *probably* have it adopted, though, so there's no need for you to worry about having to give me money every week and all that.

You don't have to go on about being sorry, I don't really blame you for what happened. It was my own stupid fault for letting you do it without using anything. We've been told often enough what might happen, it's just I didn't believe it could happen to me. (All the girls at this school I'm at say exactly the same thing. No one planned to get pregnant.)

Are you going out with anyone at the moment? Funnily enough, I'm not!

Thanks for saying that you'll come and see me in hospital but I'm not sure if I want you to. If the baby's adopted I think it will be whisked away and then I'm going to come home immediately. I would like to try and get back to normal as soon as I can.

Love, Megan

June 12th

Dear Susie,

I'm as fat as a pig. Two pigs. Although I am trying not to eat too much (and no junk, don't worry), I'm hungry all the time and walk round grazing on anything I see. My auntie says I have worn the fridge hinges out, opening it so many times.

Cathy says I really ought to try and decide soon about adoption, but I can't. I still don't believe I'm really having a baby (even though I can feel it moving all the time, and have seen the funny little thing on a scan). It still doesn't seem real; not a real baby with a name. A *person*. The babies in the unit are called Joy, Emil, Milly, Lewis and Deena. I think about names for mine, but would it keep that name if it was going to be adopted? The two names I like are Nicola if it's a girl, and Elliot if it's a boy.

Lorna hasn't asked too many questions about what I'm going to do after I've had the baby – she said to me that she didn't want to influence me either way. I *think*, though, that she thinks I ought to keep it. If I did, tell me again how long I'd have to stay in Bed and Breakfast. Is it definite that I'd have to do that? Might it be possible for me to get a flat straight away?

Lots of love, Megan

12 Armitage Road,
Chester

June 18th

Dear Miss Springer,

Thank you for your letter. Yes, I'm fine, except I keep falling asleep all the time. I've just about finished my exams now, so I'll be coming home shortly. I'm seven months now and at my last hospital visit the doctor said I might not go the full term. I can't remember why he said it; they get you in and out of there so fast that you never have time to ask questions.

I don't know what I'll be doing yet about the baby, it makes me feel a bit panicky. What I've got to settle is SO important and I don't feel up to making a decision at the moment. Sometimes I think that once I've had the baby I won't ever want to be parted from it, other times I feel I don't want the responsibility of someone else FOR EVER, and that if I keep it I'll never go to university or travel or get a good job or do any of the other things I wanted to do. It's so difficult.

Claire and I are writing to each other and she tells me all the gossip from home. I feel completely removed from that life, though. As if I'm another person now. I hope I go back to being me eventually.

Love from Megan

12 Armitage Road,
Chester

June 21st

Dear Mum,

Thought I'd let you know that the last exam went okay. All we've got to do now is wait for the results in August. (That's two reasons for dreading August.)

Looking forward to seeing you soon. Lorna is cooking me a special farewell meal next Friday and she's invited my friend Amy from the unit. I'm getting the midday train on Saturday, and Lorna says she'll ring you to confirm when she's put me on it.

Lots of love, Megan

PS: Love to Ellie. Too tired to write to her.

June 22nd

Dear Dad,

Thanks for your letter and the bank draft. Lorna has cashed it for me and I've bought some HUGE bras and knickers and a skirt and pair of trousers. I also bought some nappies and two little sleepsuits for the baby. Even if I give it up I think it ought to have some clothes of its own to go away with.

You say you have never heard anything about Lorna and a big romance. I think his name was Maurice, because when we've been talking about relationships and so on, she's mentioned him a couple of times. I think she's still sad about losing him. She said to me that she can never be totally, one hundred percent happy ever again, so that must be because of him.

Anyway, I'll be writing from home, next. And of course I'll get Mum to ring you when I have the baby.

Lots of love, Megan

12 Armitage Road
Chester

June 24th

Dear Claire,
 Thanks for your letter and Best Teachers Top Ten.
 This will be my last letter to you as I'll be seeing you soon. I'm coming back next weekend – Mum will probably have me smuggled in under cover of darkness so that none of the neighbours see me. She's told the old girl down the road that I've gone away to recover from asthma! (Ah, that must be what's making me fat.)
 Something really funny happened on Monday. I went to the cinema with my new friend Amy (who's even bigger than I am) and we got chatted up by two boys sitting in the row behind us. They bought us ice creams and we carried on talking to them during the film, and then they asked if we'd go on somewhere after, and we said yes and could hardly stop giggling. When the film finished we got up – *lumbered* to our feet – and turned to face them. You should have seen their faces! They nearly broke the door down in

their efforts to get out. Talk about laugh. I nearly went into labour there and then.

How did your last exams go? Did you have a barbecue on the last day of term? Thanks for sending me everyone's love. Give my love back to those you think ought to have it.

I've had a couple of letters from Luke now. I haven't replied to the last one yet. I know I was annoyed because he hadn't contacted me, but now that he has I've decided that it's easier *not* hearing from him. I'm scared to get too friendly with him in case he suddenly puts claims on me and says he doesn't want me to have the baby adopted. How awkward will *that* be?!

I'm so huge I can't get the seat belt in Lorna's car around me. It's been good being up here but I'll be quite pleased to get home. I've even missed my mum and Ellie, so I must be going soft in the head.

My friend Amy – talk about lucky! – invited me back to see the nursery her mum and dad have done out for her baby. It's got deep blue walls (she's been told it's a boy), a wooden floor, white rugs and white furniture painted with yellow ducks. It's *beautiful*. She's already got lots of baby clothes from Gap, including jeans and a tiny denim jacket, and a cradle that rocks. I cried

when I got home – if I was keeping my baby it wouldn't
have any of those things. It wouldn't have *anything*.

I'm OK now, though. Sort of OK.

Lots of love, Megan

June 26th

Dear Lorna,

Sorry I cried all over you at the station. I didn't mean to, but (as you know) I boo about everything these days.

You made me cry last night when you told me about why you could never be really happy. I will never *ever* tell your secret, you needn't worry. I won't say a word to Mum or Dad or even hint about it. I realise now why you haven't exactly been keen to talk about my coming baby – it must have brought it all back to you.

I want to thank you for having me up there and everything else. You didn't make me feel guilty all the time, and you didn't make me feel dirty, or as if I'd let everyone down. I promise I will think very carefully about what I'm going to do next, and I'll be in touch soon.

With all my love, Megan

CHAPTER 13

I sealed up Lorna's letter, put it in my bag, and took a quick look at the good-looking boy opposite me on the train. I was sitting in a four-seater arrangement with a table in front of me, and he was on the other side of the carriage on another four-seater. This meant we had two tables between us and he couldn't see what I was like from the waist downwards. Which was just as well.

He glanced up at me, gave a half-grin and went back to his book.

I closed my eyes. Next time the man came along selling drinks from the trolley the boy – his name was Gareth or Tim – would lean over and ask me if I wanted a coffee. Then he'd come and sit on the seat opposite me and we'd discuss what books we were reading. He was probably a student at Liverpool or somewhere and he'd be really interesting. When we got to the next big stop he'd ask me if I wanted to get off, have something to eat with him and catch a later train back. We'd go to this really nice veggie place he knew and there would be a couple of his mates there, and we'd sit around talking and they'd tell me where they'd travelled the previous year and where they were going this summer. And then Gareth would say: Hey, why don't you come along? and his mates would say: What a great idea, and they'd get out maps and we'd go over the route. Later we'd catch the last train, and Gareth and I would sit close together, looking out of the window as we flashed through neon-lit towns, and my head would rest on his shoulder and before we arrived he'd kiss me gently and beautifully and tell me he'd loved me from the moment he saw me.

In my dreams.

What would happen was that in a minute I'd have to stand up to go to the loo. He'd glance up as I heaved my hippo self past him and then he'd shrink back, horrified.

As I thought of this scenario I wriggled in my seat, knowing I'd have to get up soon; dreading it. The boy and I had already exchanged a couple of smiles and glances – not really flirting, but *something* – so a tiny little spark had already passed between us. As soon as I moved I was going to stamp that out, of course.

I sighed. It *could* happen, though. Another year on, or at some unspecified time in the future, it could – but only if I gave the baby away. If I kept the baby, then it couldn't happen. Not ever, because if I was on a train again I'd have a baby, two hundred sticky sweets, a duffel bag full of nappies, a feeding cup, a baby buggy and a set of clothes ready for when it was sick down itself. I'd never get chatted up by a good-looking student.

I looked out of the train window, wondering where we were, thinking about Lorna. The night before – well, I knew there was some mystery but I hadn't any idea what – she'd told me that she'd had a baby twenty years ago, when she was seventeen. She'd been at college then, doing a residential course, and had managed to keep it a secret from everyone at home. No one – her mum, dad or brother – ever found out. The father of the baby, Maurice, was married, and he'd dropped her like a hot potato as soon as she'd told him she was pregnant. She didn't have any money of her own, and already knew she wanted to have a proper, interesting career, so decided it was best to have her baby adopted as soon as it was born. Everyone – the social workers and so on – told her all along that it was for the good of the baby, and the best, most unselfish thing she could do.

'It wasn't the best thing I could have done for me, though,' she told me sadly. 'I never got over it. You never do. I think about my son every day of my life. It's like a terrible pain inside that never goes away.'

'But couldn't you try and find him?' I asked.

She shrugged. 'I've tried to. I've registered with an agency – they keep a list of birth mothers who want to renew contact with their children – but so far he hasn't come forward to give his name. I have to wait until he wants to make contact with me.' Her eyes had filled with tears. 'He may never do that. I expect he thinks I abandoned him – and I did!'

We both cried. Lorna for her baby, and me for mine. Also for the situation I was in and the impossibility of making the right decision.

After a while, Lorna fetched a box of tissues and we blew our noses and smiled sheepishly at each other.

'Given the time again, I'd never give my baby away,' she said. 'But you must do what's right for *you*.'

'But suppose I don't find out what's right for me until it's too late?'

'That's just it, isn't it?' She heaved a sigh. 'You just never know. I wasn't intending to tell you about what happened to me – I never ever talk about it – but then I thought if you didn't know the other side of it . . . ' her voice trailed away.

'I can't decide!' I said, panic rising. 'It's too difficult.'

'It's a bit easier now. You have more options and you'll get more help if you want to keep the baby. Twenty years ago – well, I was just a bit of a tart.' She gave a short laugh. 'I remember when I was pregnant, older women used to look at the size of me and then glance at my finger to see if I had a wedding ring. When they saw I hadn't, they gave me a disgusted look.'

'They do that now!' I said. 'That part isn't any different.'

'There was never any suggestion that I'd get a flat if I kept the baby. Not like you can.'

'So you really think I should . . . '

She shook her head. 'I don't know. Who am I to tell you to keep your baby when I've given away mine? All I know is, if you do give it away, you'll never forget this baby. It will stay with you for ever.'

As I was mulling this over again, there was an announcement from the train loudspeaker to say that we'd shortly be arriving at the next stop. When I looked over, the boy opposite – Gareth – was tugging a huge green rucksack down from the rack above him.

He turned and half-nodded at me, smiling fleetingly.

I smiled back and he went on his way, heaving his way down the carriage, his rucksack bumping along the seats.

Best way, I thought, as the train started up again. All fantasies were preserved, and I could go to the loo without worrying about it. He'd been really nice, though . . .

Mum and Ellie were at the station to meet me. To my amazement Mum came up and hugged me, and we walked out of the station to get a taxi (a taxi, no less) arm in arm. 'It's good to have you back,' she said, sounding as if she really meant it. 'Ellie and I have missed having you around. We've even missed the awful music.'

She began to get a bit anxious as we neared home, though. 'Just look at the size of you!' she said, marvelling at my tummy. 'I never remember being as big as that with you or Ellie.'

'I'm big for my dates, the doctor said.' I grinned. 'I'm quite enormous with this asthma.'

Her lips pursed, but then she smiled slightly. 'Well,

I couldn't think of what else to tell her.'

I looked out of the window at the familiar streets, pleased to be home. 'Have you seen anything of anyone? Have any teachers phoned from the school? Has Claire been round?'

Mum shook her head.

'I saw Claire with Josie last week,' Ellie said. 'They were buying suntan lotion in the chemist's. They took *ages*.'

'Susie's been in touch with me a couple of times about different things,' Mum said. 'She's coming to see you next week.' She lowered her voice. 'She said that she's going to speak to you about the adoption procedure.'

I looked at her sharply. 'I still haven't decided.'

Mum squeezed my arm. 'No, but you'll have to soon, won't you? And you know it'll be the best thing. The kindest thing you can do for your baby. You'll be giving it to two parents who'll love it, and then you can put all this behind you and get on with your life.'

Just like that, I thought. Easy peasy.

When we got in, I rang Claire's number. There was no one in, but her dad's voice on the answerphone said in a jolly voice: 'The Poretti family are on holiday. If it's urgent, please leave a message after the tone. We will be accessing this number to get our calls. Thank you very much and goodbye.'

I put the phone down and went into my room, thinking deeply. Claire was away, and it was just about the time we were supposed to have been going originally. She'd told me that the holiday wasn't on, though, because her dad couldn't get the time off work. The other thing on my mind was that Ellie had said she'd seen Claire and Josie in the chemist's, buying suntan lotion . . .

I looked up Josie's phone number, went down the hall and rang her. When her mum answered and found out it was me, she sounded as embarrassed as anything.

'Oh, hello, love,' she said. 'You're back, are you? Are you well? Not long to go now, then!'

'A month,' I said. 'Is Josie there, please?'

'I'm afraid she isn't. She . . . she's gone away with Claire. I thought you knew.'

I took a deep breath. 'Yes, I did,' I lied, 'but I wasn't sure of the date. Thanks anyway!'

I put the phone down. How *could* she? How could either of them do this to me?

I burst into tears. Sometimes I loved this baby and really wanted it, but sometimes I hated it.

It had changed my life in all sorts of ways, and I hadn't even had it yet.

CHAPTER 14

Susie hugged me. 'You've put on weight! How are you feeling? Have you been doing your antenatal exercises?'

I nodded. 'We did them in Cottesloe in the afternoons. And I've got an exercise sheet that I've sort of been following.'

'And how have things been?'

We went through to the kitchen and I put the kettle on. 'OK,' I said, 'but I'm just tired all the time. And my back aches. And I'm so *huge* – and so hot I could scream.'

'Have a cool shower,' she advised. 'When it all gets too much, go under the shower and stand there as long as you like.'

'Yeah, OK,' I said, 'but we're on a water meter. If I'm in there and running water for more than two minutes, Mum knocks on the door.'

'Go in there when she's out, then,' Susie said. She smiled sympathetically. 'And how are you in yourself, Megan?'

'Fed up.' I sighed. 'I think about it all the time – about adoption – whether I should, or whether I shouldn't. Mum seems to be taking it for granted that I'll be giving the baby up, though. All she talks about is what a relief it'll be for us afterwards, and how we can get on with our lives. She's even on about us all having a holiday abroad somewhere before I go back to school in September.' I put my arms around my tummy, rubbing the place where the baby was kicking. 'I just can't think what it will be like to go back to school. I don't even know if I want to.'

Susie nodded understandingly.

I screwed up my face. 'I think what it is, why I really can't decide what to do, is that deep down I don't believe I'm pregnant.' I patted my tummy. 'Even with this great lump, I simply *do not* believe that a real live baby is going to come out.'

Susie laughed. 'You've just got bad wind, is that it? It's blown you up.'

I made the tea and we sat down with a mug each. 'If I do decide to have it adopted,' I said slowly, 'would I see it when it was born, or would it just be whisked away?'

'Of course you'd see it!'

'And how long would I . . . I mean, suppose I changed my mind afterwards?'

'What would happen,' Susie said, 'is that the baby would go to foster parents for at least six weeks. You'd be allowed to see it all that time.'

'Would I have to?' I interrupted, not knowing whether seeing it would be worse or better.

'Whether you see it or not would be completely up to you to decide,' she said soothingly, 'whatever you felt was best. As I said, the baby would stay there for six weeks or so while we looked for a suitable couple to adopt it, and once they'd been found it would leave the foster family and go to them. That's if you hadn't changed your mind during the six weeks or so.'

'And once it was there with the new parents that would be it, would it? Would it belong to them forever?'

'Not quite,' Susie said. 'There's still a short period while all the legal procedures are carried out in which you can change your mind. It's only when the new parents have been to court and have adopted the baby legally that you can't get it back.'

I nodded slowly. 'And what if I decided right now that I *didn't* want it adopted?' I asked. 'What would happen then?'

Susie looked serious. 'I want you to understand that it will be very, very difficult for you,' she said. 'You mustn't underestimate that. A dear little sleeping baby wrapped in a shawl is one thing, a screaming toddler throwing itself on the floor is quite another. You'll be short of money, you'll probably be living somewhere grotty, a lot of your friends won't be bothered with you . . . '

' . . . Mum will disown me,' I put in.

'Maybe.'

'But I'd have the baby, wouldn't I? I'd have *someone*.'

'A baby isn't a substitute for friends and family,' Susie said. 'More than likely you would be very lonely.'

I looked at her bleakly. It wasn't sounding too good.

'What would probably happen – if you decided to keep the baby and you couldn't stay at home – is that you'd be placed in a foster home with it for a while.'

'What, you mean like a children's home?'

Susie shook her head. 'No, in a family home with an older woman who'd brought up kids of her own. While you lived there you'd have to prove to the Social Services that you were capable of taking care of a baby on your own. Once they'd decided that you could, then they'd look for hostel accommodation for you. Or bed and breakfast lodgings. And all the time you'd be monitored to make sure you were keeping suitable company, managing your money, looking after the baby properly – all those sorts of things. It's not plain sailing by any means: you don't just say you want to keep it and that's that.'

We talked some more, then Mum came in from work, Ellie came in from her friend's house and we had another pot of tea. Susie chatted to Mum in the other room for a bit, and then left.

'Susie said she talked to you about the adoption,' Mum said as soon as she'd gone.

'She talked to me about adoption,' I said. 'Not especially *the* adoption. We talked about lots of things.'

'Well, I'm glad you're seeing sense,' Mum said comfortably. 'You'd never be able to manage a child on your own. You're still only a child yourself!'

I didn't say anything because I didn't feel up to getting into a row. I wished there was someone who could make the decision for me, who could say: Megan Warrell, *this* is the right choice for you. Do this, take this path, and don't think any more about it.

That afternoon I had an antenatal appointment at the hospital. It took me ages to get there because although I caught a bus into town, when I got off I had to walk up a long hill. It was horrendously hot and I kept getting a crampy feeling underneath the lump where the baby was: every so often my tummy would tighten and twist as if there was a big elastic band pulling it together. Whenever it did this I had to stop and lean on the wall.

Once at the hospital it was like being on a conveyor belt: a whole troop of women and girls sitting on benches, all in various stages of pregnancy, taking it in turns to go into cubicles to be weighed, then measured, then blood-pressured.

Once I'd had all these things done the midwife came along to examine me. She said I was fine, but the baby was the wrong way round: lying so that it was bottom first, instead of head first. She said that the doctor might come along and try to turn it. In the end, though, I didn't see him, because he was bleeped to go up to the labour ward for an emergency.

I shuddered when I heard those words *emergency* and *labour ward* together. At Cottesloe we'd had lots of talks on giving birth, and been shown a video with a woman smiling in an exhausted way at the camera while a baby forced its way out down below. I hadn't been fooled by the smile. I knew that childbirth was going to be the most painful thing in the world – even if I had an epidural. Amy had been terrified of it, too, but she had painful periods and thought it was a reasonable exchange: labour = period pains × nine.

When I was leaving the clinic I glanced along the row of women still waiting, hoping I might see someone about my own age. There was a girl bending over, trying to pull a toddler out from under a chair, shouting at him. When she stood up, I saw that it was Izzy Clark, the girl who'd been at my school. So she wasn't in Leeds with twins. She *was* hugely pregnant again, though.

She straightened up and looked at me. I smiled at her tentatively. 'You used to go to my school.'

'Did I?' She sounded as if she couldn't care less. She looked fat and frumpy and was wearing what looked like slippers on her feet.

'My name's Megan Warrell. You probably don't remember me.'

'But you remember me, right? Famous for getting hounded out of school!' She smiled bitterly. 'Joined the club, have you?'

I nodded. 'My baby's due next month.'

'The best of bloody luck.'

'This is your little girl, is it?' I pulled a funny face at the toddler, trying to make her laugh. 'She's sweet.'

She wasn't, actually. She had something red and

sticky round her mouth, her T-shirt was dirty and a wet nappy drooped between her legs.

'She's a right little cow,' Izzy said feelingly.

I didn't know what to say to this. 'When's your next one due?' I asked.

'End of September.' She looked up at me. 'You still with the bloke who got you pregnant?'

I shook my head. 'Are you?'

'You're joking. They scarpered – both of them.'

'So . . . Do you work, or what?'

'How can I work? Who's going to look after her? Who'd look after *two* kids?'

'Your mum?' I asked.

She made a dismissive noise. 'Threw me out, didn't she? Her new bloke did, anyway.'

'Didn't you want to go back to school?'

'No fear!'

I hesitated. 'Are you having another baby to be company for this one?' I asked. What I actually meant was, why was she having another baby when she did-n't seem to like the first one?

She shrugged. 'It's something to do,' she said. 'I'm at home with this one, so I thought I might as well have another one and make it worthwhile. You get more money.'

170

Oh God, I thought. I smiled at her bleakly. 'Where are you living?'

'In a block of flats on Sydney Street. Fourth floor – no lift,' she said. 'I'd ask you over but it's a pigsty.'

'Perhaps I could give you a ring sometime,' I said, thinking that any friend would be better than no friend. And at least, if I kept the baby (*was I keeping the baby?*) Izzy would know the ropes.

'Are you in the phone book?' I asked.

She pulled a face. 'You don't get in the phone book if you haven't got a phone.'

I wanted to ask her loads more things: what she did with herself all day, did she have friends, did she go out, how did she manage, what happened when she met boys – did she tell them? – but just then a nurse came out the front and called her name.

'See you!' Izzy said. She yanked the toddler to its feet and went towards one of the cubicles, her slippers flopping up and down as she walked. She had a nasty purple vein at the back of her leg, I noticed.

I sat down on the edge of the bench, preparing myself for the walk back to the bus stop. Izzy: well, that was how you got if you kept your baby. You got miserable and crabby, and you got poor. A couple of the girls at Cottesloe had been a bit like that, but I

171

hadn't known what they'd been like to start with. I could remember Izzy, though. She'd been pretty and sparky, always giggling. And now she wasn't. OK, she had a baby – but that was the only thing she *did* have. Suppose she'd been like Lorna and given her baby away, would she be happier now?

When I got back from the hospital, Mum was in. She asked me what had happened there and I told her about the baby being the wrong way up, but didn't tell her about Izzy.

A bit later, when she'd gone out to the kitchen, Ellie said in a low voice that someone had come round for me.

'Who?' I said. 'Why didn't Mum tell me?'

'I was watching telly and she went to the door,' Ellie said in a conspiratorial whisper – she'd been much nicer to me since I'd been away. 'She came back and said it was just someone selling something, but I know it wasn't. I saw him from the window.'

'Saw who?'

'Luke!' Ellie said. 'Mum told him a lie – she said you weren't back from Lorna's yet.'

'Oh, *did* she?'

'Don't tell her I told you!' Ellie whispered. 'Promise?'

172

I nodded. I didn't much care, anyway. I didn't want to see Luke. All he'd do was mess things up in my head even more.

The baby stirred and I rocked backwards and forwards, trying to calm it down, hoping it would turn round the right way. I'd heard about breech births; knew they were much more difficult than ordinary ones.

Trust *you*, I said to the baby. Trust you to be bloody awkward. And then I asked it straight out: What am I going to do with you? Do you want to stay with me, or do you want a proper home with a mum and a dad? Kick once for adoption, twice for staying with me.

There was no more kicking, but the elastic band inside me pulled and tightened. I groaned and rolled over onto my side on the sofa, trying to get more comfortable.

'What's up?' Ellie said urgently. 'Are you all right?'

'Yeah. Fantastic,' I said. No one was going to make the decision for me, let alone the baby. I had to work things out for myself.

CHAPTER 15

'You tell her.'
'No, *you* tell her.'
'She knows, anyway. My mum told her.'
'What d'you think she'll say?'
It was Claire and Josie, coming along the balcony of the flats. It was another sweltering day and I was lying on the sofa in the front room, under the wide open window, trying to get some air. I'd just written to Dad again, telling him all the latest and promising again that Mum would ring as soon as I had the baby.

I lay still, listening to Claire and Josie outside.
'Well, anyhow she couldn't expect . . . ' Claire began.
'Yes, she could!' Josie hooted. 'She *is* expecting!'
They rang the door, giggling.
'What I mean,' Claire said in a low voice, 'is that she couldn't seriously expect my mum and dad to take her on holiday when she's eight months pregnant, could she?'

I thought about not answering the door, but only for a second. I'd have to see them sooner or later, and anyway, I craved contact with ordinary people, some sort of normality, some *friends*. Even if it was just them going on about the holiday they'd had without me.

They rang again and I gently rolled onto the floor, onto my hands and knees, then knelt and got up. I'd discovered it was the best way of getting to my feet.

On my way to the door I thought about looking at myself in the mirror, but I didn't. I knew I looked horrendous: like a great toad.

We all said our hellos in an embarrassed way. 'Look at the size of you! I bet you're having twins!' Josie said, and I pretended I hadn't heard this before and laughed. Neither of them, I was pleased to say, looked a bit brown.

'Sorry about the holiday,' Claire said, hanging back as I closed the door behind them. 'But my dad honestly didn't think he could get the time off and then he could, but you were away and . . . '

'It doesn't matter.'

'It rained most of the time, anyway,' Claire said. She added in a whisper, 'And Josie wasn't as much fun as you.'

I carried on into the front room, pretending I hadn't heard but pleased all the same.

'What's been happening round here, then?' I asked when we were all sitting down. 'What's the gossip?'

'Well . . . ' Claire said, and she launched into a complicated story about an argument between Naomi and Vinny, and then Josie went on to tell me about this boy she'd met on holiday (while Claire rolled her eyes at me) and then they talked about GCSEs and the Sixth Form and how they were going to *die* waiting for the results, and finally they ran out of stories.

When I tried to think about their visit later, I could hardly remember anything they'd said. It had washed over me like a tide and gone away again. It was as if I was in a little cocoon: just me and the baby. I didn't belong in their world, the world of school and summer holidays and clothes and bands and boys, any more.

'What about you, then?' Josie asked eventually. 'How you feeling?'

'Has Luke been round to see you?' said Claire.

I shot a look at her. I was sure she fancied him. *Certain* of it. That was another thing I couldn't really be bothered to think about, though. Who cared?

'He's been round,' I said, 'but Mum didn't tell me. And he wrote to me a few times when I was away.'

'Did he say anything about the baby?' Claire asked.

I shook my head. 'Not really.'

'He's worried about his A levels,' Claire went on. 'He's only going to get into University if he gets good grades. If he doesn't, his dad's sending him to another school, to do retakes.'

'Oh,' I said. One of my recent daydreams had involved him coming to see me in hospital and saying that he wanted to help me take care of the baby, and of him getting a flat somewhere for me and the baby and coming to take us out at weekends. Now he was definitely going away.

'I expect his dad's moving him away from you!' said Josie.

'Yeah,' I said bitterly. 'I'm a terrible influence.'

'What's happening about the baby now, then?' Claire said. 'Are you going to keep it or what?'

I shrugged. 'Don't know.'

'You still don't know!' Claire said. 'You're practically *having* it and you still don't know!'

'Keep it!' Josie urged. 'Babies are cool. My cousin's got a baby and she wears one of those stretchy coloured hairbands and a little gold earring. Guess what her name is?!'

We tried to guess but had to give up.

'It's Mango!' Josie shrieked. 'Honestly! My cousin said she called her Mango because she's so gorgeous she could eat her!'

I smiled, though the tightening was happening again, harder than ever, quite vicious, and it took a huge effort.

'Mango wears these really wild things: tie-dyed stuff and silk scarves instead of dresses – things like that.'

I heaved a sigh as the pain went away again. 'I don't know what to do,' I said. 'I can't decide.'

'What's your mum like now? Is she all right about it?' Claire asked.

'My mum would go *ballistic!*' Josie put in.

I shrugged. 'She's all right . . . but only because she thinks I'm having the baby adopted.'

'Just tell her you want to keep it,' Josie said airily. 'Go on – it'd be great!'

There was a silence. 'I don't know if it will,' I said. 'I can't make up my mind.'

'We'd come round and see you, wouldn't we, Claire?'

Claire nodded. 'We'd babysit for you.'

'If you were doing the babysitting I wouldn't have anyone to go out with,' I pointed out.

'Can I get myself a drink?' Josie said suddenly. 'Water would be OK. I'm dry as anything.'

'I'll get it,' I said. 'There are some cold drinks in the fridge.' I thought it best not to roll onto the floor to get to my feet, so I put my arms behind me and pushed myself up. I took one step towards the kitchen and then something happened. Something *drastic*. I burst into tears of fright and sat down again.

'What's up?' Claire said.

'I . . . think . . . my waters have gone!' I said in a hoarse voice.

'What's that mean?' Josie said.

'You know!' Claire said in a panic. 'The bag of water that the baby's in – it breaks when you go into labour – when you're about to give birth.'

Josie gave a short scream. 'Is it all gushing out? Ugggh!'

'What shall I do?' Claire asked urgently. 'Shall I ring your mum?'

I nodded, sitting on the edge of the sofa, frightened to move an inch or look down to see what had happened. 'Her number's by the phone. Quickly!'

Claire ran out and Josie sat, turned to stone, looking at me in horror, as if I was going to have the baby right then on the carpet in front of her.

180

I put my thumb in my mouth and rocked back-wards and forwards. It was all too soon. I hadn't had enough time to get used to it, I didn't know what I was going to do with it. I didn't want it yet; not until I'd decided.

I felt a sharp pain which left me gasping for breath and I struggled to remember: breathing, pain control, relaxation. Whether I wanted it or not, the baby was coming right now . . .

CHAPTER 16

I opened my eyes and stared up at neon strip lights on the ceiling.

My hands clenched and unclenched. Beneath them I felt smooth sheets and underneath, smoother plastic. Where was I?

'Hello, my love!' There was a nurse by my side, rubbing my hand. 'Megan! Are you awake?'

'Is it over?' I licked my lips. My mouth felt like dust, there was a drip going into my right arm and I had a huge dull ache in the area of my tummy.

'Yes, it's all over and you've got your baby.'

'Ah,' I breathed, remembering. 'Is it all right?'

'It's beautiful!' The nurse stood beside me, smiling. 'Do you know where you are? Can you remember what happened?'

'My waters went and I came into hospital . . . ' I croaked.

'You were in labour for a while and the baby was up the wrong way, so the doctors decided to give you a

Caesarean. You've just come round from the anesthetic and you're doing well. We've just got to get your blood pressure down a little, then you can go onto the ward.'

I lifted my head and looked beside the bed. There was no sign of any cot in the room. Why was this? Was there something wrong? 'Where's the baby?' I asked urgently.

'Next door in the baby unit, having a rest.'

'Can I see it?'

'Of course you can. I'll help you to sit up, and then bring it in for a cuddle.'

I tried to clear my head. Was I still dreaming? No, this was real. This was me, in hospital, with a baby that I was going to see right *now*.

I'd had the baby.

It was here.

The strong arm of the nurse came round me, pulling me into a sitting position. Pillows were arranged behind me and the drip was moved over my shoulder so that it wasn't in the way.

The nurse went off and, a minute later, came back with a bundle wrapped in a white cotton hospital blanket. My heart started thumping with an unbelievable excitement. This was a baby. I'd had it and it was mine. All mine.

'Here we are!' she said. She smiled at me. 'There's something you haven't asked me yet.'

My head was filled with muzziness. I couldn't think. I was nearly all there, almost back with the world, but not quite. 'Is it OK?'

'You've already asked *that*!'

She put the bundle into my arms. 'Most new mums want to know whether they've had a boy or girl.'

I looked down at the baby, at the smooth pink cheeks, the dark, downy head, the spiky lashes. I felt – oh, as if I recognised him. As if I knew my baby already. As if there was something which had fastened us together with invisible, unbreakable ties. 'It's a boy,' I said, my eyes filling with tears.

'Good guess!' She fitted my baby more snugly into my arms, then backed off. 'I'll leave you to get to know each other for a few minutes, and then I'll go along and get your mum from the waiting room and we can all have a cuppa.'

I hardly heard her, I was so intent on looking at my baby. A few minutes! I felt that even if I looked at him from now till forever I could never look enough. My baby. My own baby.

And suddenly, *suddenly*, it all fell into place. All the things I'd been thinking, all the different paths I could take, all my doubts, disappeared. I didn't know what would happen, how I'd manage, but one thing was suddenly crystal clear: nothing on earth would make me part with this baby. *Nothing*.

What will Megan do?
Watch out for the sequel

$$(megan)^2$$

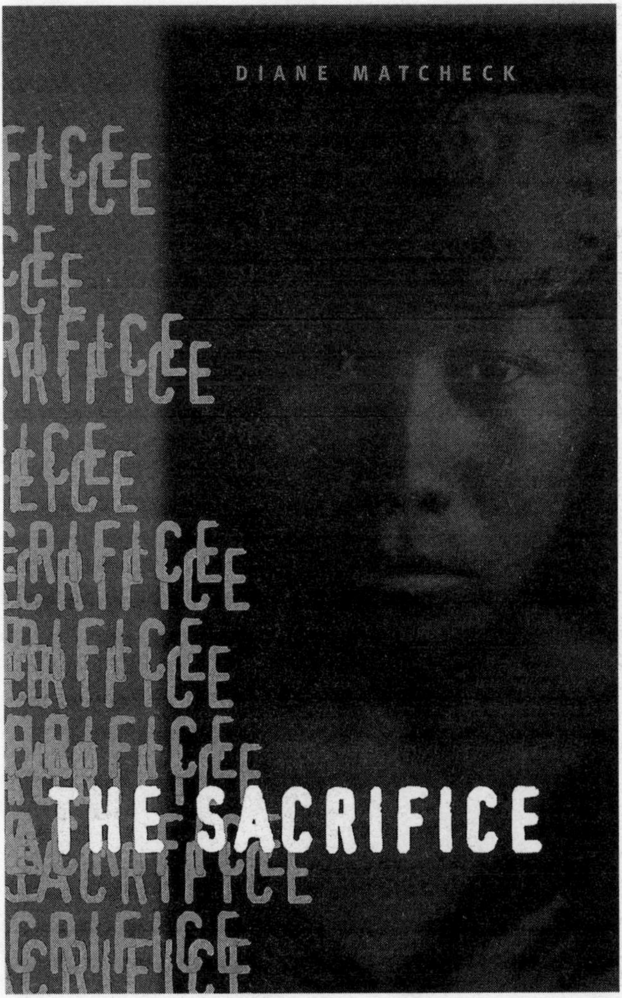
DIANE MATCHECK
THE SACRIFICE